UNHOLY WARRIOR

Rebecka Jäger

Unholy Warrior

copyright © 2020 by Rebecka Jäger

Any references to historical events, real people, or real places are used fictitiously. Names, characters, and places are products of the author's imagination.

First printing edition 2020. Self-published   The author's website: www.rebeckajager.com

Rebecka Jäger on social media:
Blog on writing and book marketing: https://rebeckajager.com/blog/
Facebook: https://www.facebook.com/rebeckajagerwriter/
Twitter: https://twitter.com/JagerWriter/
Pinterest: https://fi.pinterest.com/rebeckajager/
Instagram: https://www.instagram.com/rebeckajager/
Medium: https://medium.com/@rebecka.jager
Linkedin: https://medium.com/@rebecka.jager
Goodreads: https://www.goodreads.com/author/show/18534349/
BookBub: https://www.bookbub.com/profile/rebecka-jager
Allauthor: https://allauthor.com/author/rebeckajager/

Book design by Aidana WillowRaven

ISBN-13 paperback: 978-952-94-3700-9
ISBN-13 hardcover: 978-952-94-3701-6
ISBN-13 pdf: 978-952-94-3702-3
ISBN-13 epub: 978-952-94-3703-0

Dedication

I dedicate this book to my ever-patient husband, who wishes to remain unnamed. And to my writer friend Stephanie Colbert who offered the best of critique.

Contents

Prologue

Second lieutenant Rebane Nordstrom knelt in the packed snow. She let her index finger rest against the trigger guard of the 9mm Grach Yarygin because her hands wouldn't stop shaking. Her spotter, Daniil Kowalski, moved, and the fabric of his snow parka made crackling sounds. Blood from his wound had soaked through and it was frozen stiff. She held his gaze for a long moment, but Daniil's tanned features expressed no advice.

"Say something, Daniil," she whispered. "You know what the enemy will do to me."

Daniil shifted his weight. He still held onto his assault rifle, although the magazine was empty. "Let's take our chances, Reb," he suggested after a frown. "It's a long way to the front line. Perhaps they'll let their guard down during transport, and we can run."

He grunted from pain as he tried to sling the rifle over his shoulder. Rebane holstered her pistol and rose with stiff knees to help him, wrapping his rime-coated muzzle behind him. He had to be in terrible pain from the bullet still lodged between his ribs.

Before Daniil could reach for a last kiss, Ivanov, the resistance liaison officer, and a mountain of a man from Kazakhstan, emerged atop the ridge. He held the cotter pin of the last grenade between his fingers, ready to pull, and fire burned in his eyes. "We should blow ourselves to pieces right now!" he shouted. "Don't let the enemy get you," he added as Rebane stared at him.

"Ruki vverh – Lift up your hands!" A hoarse voice sounded from the mist before Rebane could object. A Union captain stepped forth as a silhouette against the pallid sky. "You're surrounded from all sides. Lower your weapons to the ground now," he yelled in his inept Russian.

Rebane opened the buckle of her gun belt and kneeled. Soldiers of the European Union rolled forth like links in a chain, and Ivanov let go of the grenade. The enemy wore their usual winter camouflage which blurred with the wet ground and patches of snow.

How the hell did they know where to find us?

She descended the hillside frog-marched between two privates. They had cuffed her wrists and patted her down. Gone was her double-bladed knife which she housed on her ankle holster at all times. The captain chased his peaked cap downhill after a gust stole it from him. She seized the opportunity to look over her shoulder and saw Daniil struggling to walk.

Rebane's raven hair messed into a bird's nest, and she squinted through the snowflakes the wind hurled at her. On the lay-by of the mountain road below, three military trucks puffed diesel smoke into the cold air. Rebane watched Daniil climb into the first truck and couldn't shake the premonition that she might not see him again. His trouser leg had soaked through with blood.

The smell of his wounds stayed with Rebane as the pimple-faced enemy sergeant helped her into the last vehicle and seated Ivanov opposite her. She met the gaze of this chained brown bear for a passing second and knew the Kazakh would die for her if she asked for his life.

PART I

1.
On the Road

"Bastards," Rebane said under her breath as she felt the weight of the guard who leaned against her. The army truck groaned when it battled the crest of the dune. The tarp flapped open, leaving her with a view of the road as she memorized the way back east. She pinched her lips together in frustration. Her task was impossible with the everchanging landscape.

Out of the corner of her eye, she glimpsed Ivanov and caught him doing the same. Rebane looked straight ahead, not wanting to reveal signs of weakness to her captors. As the convoy reached below the tree line, branches scraped the truck's tarpaulin and rattled like bullets. Her soldier's instinct made Rebane duck. She straightened her posture the moment she understood she had overreacted. A veil of snow still slithered across the icy road, trying to snare them between the hills.

Nervous, she chewed the lining of her mouth. A sudden bump slammed her teeth together, causing the metallic taste of blood to dribble on her tongue. The handcuffs scraped Rebane's skin, and she wiggled her fingers to keep the remaining blood flow going. One of the Union men lit a cigarette, and she watched the smoke waft in the air forming a perfect circle. It took a lot of practice to accomplish that feat, and she wondered if his youthful looks were deceiving. He steadied an old M-16 assault rifle between his knees. She fixated her eyes on the weapon. All she needed was a minute before the sons-of-bitches would lie unmoving at her feet and the sickeningly sweet smell of blood filled the air.

The enemy used whatever weapons their gunsmiths could put back together, and they weren't always accurate or dependable. Dog-eat-dog skirmishes between the Union and the Russian Federation had gone on for twenty-five years—ever since the nuclear war had obliterated ninety percent of the population. The hunger in the soldier's eyes made Rebane shift on the hard surface of the bench. She became suddenly conscious of her appearance—a Nenets woman from Siberia, thirty years old and dirty as a stray dog.

You bet I stink!

Her winter camouflage was twice her size and made her look heavier. Before the enemy had captured her, she had tugged her fur cap under the wide leather belt which reached several times around her waist. She looked alien to these German and English boys. No doubt he assumed she came from China by the looks of her. The soldier's mouth hung open now, and his cigarette landed on the frozen pellet. Rebane watched the glow die.

"How long?" she asked in German. "Before we arrive?" But he stayed mute, so she repeated the question in English.

The sergeant thrust his elbow between the private's ribs to knock him out of his trance. "You don't tell that bitch anything," he ordered. "Shut the fuck up."

She suspected the Union guards had no idea who'd they'd seized on that frozen hill in Poland because they hadn't beaten or raped her. The enemy hated the likes of Rebane more than tanks; every sniper who got caught was hung from the nearest lamppost or branch within minutes. Rebane, Daniil and Ivanov belonged to the *Spetznaz*–the elite of the GRU, Russia's Military Intelligence Agency. The three of them were all that remained of the special ODON task force. Any Union fighter who brought home such a treasure would receive a promotion on the spot.

Rebane shivered, and her face felt numb. She craved water and food but didn't show what the enemy considered a weakness. Ivanov looked unaffected as always. His size made the guards wary, and they kept their distance from him. Rebane tried to sense if they traveled south or west, but the sun never emerged from the ashen clouds to signal direction. Blades of long grass ruffled in the wind that whipped the ground without respite. The layer of snow grew thinner, and Rebane knew they'd entered Hunger Country.

I might never see home again...or Daniil.

Exhaustion forced her to surrender as the rattling of the spiked tires against the tarmac became constant. Between wake and sleep, Rebane hallucinated about the blazing sunset of her childhood in Siberia. The blue mirage of the arctic magic hour cocooned her. She smelled the ozone and felt the tug of the north wind in her hair.

No! Don't fall asleep.

Startling awake, she straightened her posture. Bleak flakes landed on the soldiers' long coats, and Rebane tasted them between her teeth. The Union men placed scarves over their faces, but the prisoners could only hope for the air to clear in a few miles. This was the ash from burned cities and vaporized bodies. Thankfully, the wind turned and lifted the clouds which had poisoned the earth's atmosphere since WWIII.

A magenta bubble appeared on the horizon. Soon, another one joined the string of transparent gems and dusk grew into darkness. As they drew closer, Rebane saw that they were enormous greeneries where UV-lights and sprinklers switched on. The enemy guarded the conservatories, and numerous roadblocks slowed the convoy. Refugees rambled in the middle of the road like zombies. They didn't mind the honking of horns, but the crack of rifle bullets swooshing above their heads divided the crowd like water. The second truck closed in on Rebane's transport, and its headlights revealed the sunken faces of children dragged onward by famished adults. A lump rose into her throat.

The skeletal animals—horses, donkeys, and mules—were too weak to make a sound, and Rebane pitied them. The ruin of mankind didn't exclude animals who had no cause in the war. Wild dogs snarled as they paced beside the equines, waiting for the weakest to collapse so they could assuage their own hunger. Helpless to do anything, Rebane wished the beasts of burden would find fresh grass. And the dogs…Rebane loved all canines. She had tamed foxes since she was five.

A net fence appeared from nowhere, embellished with bullet-ridden signs of radioactivity. The entrance through the old city wall went through a checkpoint and the convoy stopped. Soldiers wearing tactical gear examined the live cargo with experienced movements. They pointed at the prisoners with rifle barrels and heavy-duty flashlights. A sour taste dwelled in Rebane's mouth as her first rough-handed interrogation drew nearer. Drops of moisture gathered on her chapped upper lip. She wanted to take off the padded winter jacket but sure as hell wouldn't ask the guards to strip her. Every inch of her body felt vulnerable as she saw the hotel's crumbling facade. Invading armies often turned such places into military offices. The enemy team erupted from the truck with their catch.

A private helped her step down onto the street. "Mind the stairs," he said with a friendly voice as the dim hotel lobby devoured them.

She found the others standing next to the wall. Rebane inched closer to Daniil, whose handsome features were distorted with pain. He avoided looking at her and a sting impaled her heart.

Don't let the prisoners plan a common pretense. Rule number one.

Their sides brushed and a jolt of energy went through Rebane's muscles. SERE rules ordered her to grab the first opportunity to escape, but wounded Daniil would slow her down. The steadfast pact of never leaving a comrade behind was now impossible to fulfill.

The Union battlefield reconnaissance had their hands full. Most of the prisoners were Russian soldiers from different platoons and Polish resistance fighters who wore scruffy civilian clothes. While the others went through the initial interview, Rebane studied the Headquarters. The marble statue of the huntress Diana stood beneath the grand stairway, a discarded piece of art. Plush carpets muffled the military bustle and faded cherubs stared at her with gentle eyes from the fresco. Armed soldiers in leaf green walked with a brisk gait, running errands and escorting prisoners to the second floor. A group of determined officers wearing SWAT black manned the sorting desks. Fatigue ached in her shins and pressed on her shoulders.

"Second Lieutenant Nordstrom?" A tall, pimple-faced sergeant addressed her. He held a pile of cardboard POW tags.

"Yes," she replied. Rebane repeated her name and rank and added her birthday.

That's all you'll get.

This string bean of a sergeant produced a form which contained her 9mm and the commando knife, which she already missed. Rebane reminded him of her assault rifle but omitted the sniper rifle she'd used in the Company job. When the siege ring had become watertight, she'd dug a hole in the frosty earth with much effort and had covered the burial ground with leaves and slush.

She slumped against the wall.

"Don't do that," the string bean leaned into whisper. "They'll make me beat you and I don't want to do that to a girl. Stand at attention."

Rebane obeyed. He shrugged before he hung the cord around her neck. She amused herself by reading the tag letters upside down.

Date and Time of Capture: 3.8.2048 at 3:48am. Serial No: 34 611FNB, Female, Rebane Nordstrom. Date of Birth: 5.12.2018. Rank: Second Lieutenant. Unit of the EPW: Arctic troops, Unit AU-157 of the Russian Federation Army, Capturing Unit: ADG15, European Union Battlefield Reconnaissance 1A. Location of Capture: Prague Strip, EU Zone 3. Grid Coordinates: WS 76670869, MJ 44LI 3657

She hadn't had a phone where she'd grown up and the unfamiliar trill always startled her. It rang until one of the senior officers, a major, took the call. It rang again after he placed the handset down and the buzzing irritated Rebane. Papers and files piled on his counter underneath a green-shaded lamp. The burly man in his late forties sat hunched until he sensed her gaze. His metal-rimmed glasses gleamed as their eyes met. The lightning of fear shot through her.

Shit! Don't make eye contact. Rule number two and you just broke it.

Daniil formed a silent curse and Rebane echoed it with a hiss. The large man rose to talk with his assisting officer, who pointed at her. Ivanov followed what happened. The brown bear's brows furrowed as the enemy duo approached and she bit her lip.

This is it. Stand your ground.

A giant of a man, the major made the petite Rebane appear to shrink in size. Her eyes followed the seams of his trousers and across the immaculate uniform jacket. She clasped her knees together.

What a pompous asshole.

His black name tag spelled WEISSER in white, all caps. He had the tabs of a major on his hard collar and expected her to salute his rank, but Rebane forced her lips to remain pursed while the bastard weighed her up for interrogation. A strap locked the Glock on his belt holster in place. If only she could get her cuffed hands in front... She buried her nails into the flesh of her palms to endure Weisser's expressionless stare.

Minutes marched by while the heavy man estimated Rebane and calculated the odds. Was it because of her sex that she would be the weakest link—high-knowledge and low-resistance? The captain beside him had already shifted his feet and looked at his wristwatch for the fifth time. Rebane thought of a knee kick into the major's groin. How easy would it be to run into the cold night, to disappear across the dark fields?

Weisser reached for the cardboard tag hanging around her neck and adjusted his glasses. "Nice to meet you, Miss Nordstrom," he said in a shadeless voice.

2.
Dogs

Rebane had no idea if she'd cleared the test or not. Behind the desk, jowly-faced Weisser continued his initial task of filing reports as if nothing had interrupted his concentration. The major never again looked at her, and Rebane forced herself into thinking the immediate danger was over. She glanced at Daniil, who kept his eyes fixed on a point in the opposite wall. He stood straight-backed with his legs spread. Rebane wondered how much blood Daniil could lose.

You were always the tough one.

Personal allegiances could be powerful tools at the hands of interrogators, and she had no intention of making their job easier. A surveillance camera at the end of a rusty lever observed the thinning crowd of prisoners. The opaque lens zoomed in on her and Rebane returned its stare. Two MPs descended the stairs. She braced herself as they came straight for her.

Both men took hold of her elbows and forced her up the stairs. On the second floor, they passed doors marked with golden numbers. Rebane imagined how the place must have looked before the wars of the 21st century had mowed everything to the ground. The once luxurious hotel seemed unprepared to function as a prison. The wallpaper was dog-eared, and the rug almost trampled her with a treacherous fold.

Fox Spirit, let the windows open without resistance. May the doors be made of rotten wood.

Dust from the explosions rested on the stairway railing. A series of bullet holes in the wall bore witness of the battle which must have raged in this Polish frontier city. The blonde MP who looked as if he was fifteen smiled at her and prompted Rebane to speak.

"I'm hungry," she said in Russian, but his face remained blank. Because she couldn't use her hands to gesture, she tried anew. "Etwas zu essen?"

"Nicht jetzt—not yet," the stocky military policeman who looked as if he enjoyed being in charge replied before the youngster could say yes.

After a few trials, he found the key which fitted the lock of room 103. "Turn around," he ordered, and his obedient pair checked Rebane's handcuffs.

She *neverminded* the other prisoner in the room and lowered herself onto the filthy floor as soon as the door closed. Squirming her arms below her butt was easy for a nimble person. Rebane unlaced her left boot to produce a hairpin from her sock, but the cuff lock resisted cooperation. Sweat broke from her pores, but her movements were swift and professional. Her cellmate raised a bushy eyebrow when her bracelet chinked open, and Rebane rubbed her bruised wrists.

"Well done," he whispered.

"You speak Russian?" she asked.

The Forest Brother from the Polish resistance nodded with a grin that revealed two of his front teeth were missing. His grey eyes scanned every inch of her. The Pole sat on the floor with his rope-bound hands on his lap.

"Why the hell didn't they cuff you?" she asked with envy in her voice.

"It must be my personality."

Great. A comedian.

Rebane decided to interview the native. A few minutes of delay could earn valuable intel. She knelt to free him and introduced herself with a whisper. "I'm Rebane."

"Arkady," he replied and eyed the tabs on her collar. "Hmm, a second lieutenant and fucking all. That could never happen to a skirt on our side."

Rebane ignored the sexist comment and asked, "How long to the front?"

"Eighteen miles, but there's a division of Union tanks progressing into Russian soil near Gdansk. The front may move eastward soon. The big offensive started after the assassination of the European Union president."

She didn't comment but felt a sting in her heart.

"A great shot—a professional, or so they tell me," Arkady added, observing her reaction with keen eyes.

"Really?" She shrugged. Sometimes the enemy placed informants among fresh POWs. "Do they have dogs?" she asked.

"I don't hear any barking. Why? Are you going to run, sis?"

Outside, a siren wailed to signal an impending airstrike. As Arkady turned his head to listen, she noticed his battered profile, his nose broken in two places.

"I'll take my chances here," he decided and reached for a cigarette pack from his flea-infested coat. The musky room filled with the pause until the siren sounded again.

Rebane gazed out of the window. Two machine-gun posts guarded the gate and searchlights sliced the velvet sky. She gestured for Arkady to help. He steadied her as she stood on the windowsill. As she had anticipated, the narrow ventilation window above the bigger glass pane wasn't locked. The rusty hinges squeaked and the chill night air entered the room. Both she and her cellmate were petrified to listen if the guards would return, but nothing moved in the corridor. Cold sweat beaded her forehead. The siren sounded the all-clear. Rebane tried to mount the frame but couldn't fit through the window with her winter garments on. She stepped down to remove her leather belt and the padded jacket, which she placed on Arkady's shoulder.

They tried anew. Rebane knew her good luck would run out any minute. She drew up her weight with her muscular arms.

"Wow," Arkady commented when she squirmed on top of the structure and extended her legs on the outside. Her feet searched for a steady hold until her boots met the narrow ledge. Arkady handed her the jacket and Rebane steeled herself to put more weight on the concrete structure.

If the ledge breaks now, I'm dead.

The freezing wind blew her long hair across her face. Rebane held onto the window frame with one hand and placed the other through the jacket sleeve. She switched handholds and prayed.

Mielikki, the Goddess of the Forest, don't let me drop anything onto the yard.

A splinter of wood stabbed her finger. Rebane swallowed the pain and gazed into the void. Falling from the second floor would sever her spine. The moon hid behind the clouds and a blanket of darkness smothered every detail. Desperation crept into her mind.

Moon, show yourself.

But the silver disc didn't take orders from humans. Rebane's fingers grew numb while she waited for the light to reappear. Straightening her arms would allow some rest, but she didn't trust the frame enough to put her full weight on it. After an everlasting minute, the coldhearted moon divided the clouds to reveal that the ledge continued around the corner. The ancient masonry allowed Rebane to place her fingers between the tiles. Glued against the wall, she advanced with quivering baby steps until the gate parted to let a black Mercedes slide through. Rebane froze as her heart tried to leap out of her mouth.

She watched the driver step out to open the passenger door and smelled the smoke before the ember of a cigarette glowed straight below her. The men chattered in hushed German and laughed. All they had to do was look up for the moonlight to reveal the silhouette of an escaped prisoner. Rebane's heartbeat quickened until the light from the hotel lobby swallowed the men.

She saw a square roof nine feet below her. It was an adjacent lower building. The moon cowered again, but Rebane dropped into the unknown with flexed knees. Upon impact, she rolled to her side and waited for her breathing to level.

Two shadows stretched on the porch stairs—guards on their smoking break. The muscular form of a German shepherd appeared between the men.

No!

The dog tensed before it released a bark that echoed across the yard. It must have picked her scent. But the cold wind came to Rebane's rescue. The men wanted to return indoors. They ordered the dog to fucking shut up and dragged him to the lobby by the harness. The door closed with a bang and shut the light inside. Darkness conquered the courtyard.

The rest was easy. When Rebane reached the street level, she buttoned her uniform jacket and hopped across the pavement. She melted into shadows behind the next house, and gravel rattled beneath her boots. Her breath formed into puffy clouds as she ran to gain distance before the search patrol traced her foot-prints. After a mile or two, Rebane stopped to scoop snow into her mouth. The cold descended into her stomach when she launched into a run again. Over a picket fence and across a sleepy yard behind a family house and she was outside the city. Relief spread into her body.

Puddles splashed as she sprang across a cropped field. The bushes shuffled at the edge of the forest, and her breathing echoed in her ears. Rebane knew she'd left a trail of scent with every step, but there wasn't enough time to make rabbit loops. Dawn already painted the horizon. She only had a few hours to find a hid-ing place. A jump over the ditch fell short and she stumbled onto her knees, curs-ing. Her right boot submerged and filled with icy water.

"Fuck!"

Between startled heartbeats, she picked up an approaching sound. Rebane halted to listen among the morning mist which wrapped its tendrils above the low ground. The wind pressed the frosty grass against her shins as she tried to identify the sharp voices, now sounding closer. She held her breath.

Dogs. Fucking barking dogs!

She sprinted toward the dawning light. Where could she find shelter? The coal cellars, the yard shacks, and the outhouses of the city were far behind her.

Have I forgotten my training?

A wall of thorny bushes tore her clothing but Rebane forced herself through. She gasped for air when she reached a patch of fir trees and the foliage hid her from view.

The yelping is louder. They're gaining on me.

She picked up speed, ignoring the sting in her side. Rebane hopped downhill between the oaks and birches and almost collided with the stone wall behind the vegetation. No use trying to climb. She couldn't get a grip on the frozen stones. The sound of her heartbeat thrashed in her ears.

Left or right?

She turned left just as the first dog leaped through the air. Rebane extended her arms for cover as the dog rammed her. She grabbed the Doberman's collar to keep the mouthful of teeth from ripping out her throat. Another set of jaws bit into her elbow and agony shot through her arm. The dogs trashed their prey, pinned it down as their handlers had trained them. The patrol couldn't be far away, and all Rebane could do was scream.

3.
Firing Squad

Rebane had measured the dimensions of her cell a thousand times—five steps to the door and less from side-to-side. Not much room for self-defense. She went through various torture scenarios while sitting on the bunk and leaning against the cool whitewashed wall. The wool blanket offered some comfort, but the uncertainty of Daniil's fate left her sleepless. There'd been no sign of him or Ivanov after she'd been caught. No chance of escape, either, because the enemy had transferred her to a maximum-security facility. Rebane grabbed a fistful of dust particles that danced in the light. Dawn peeked in through the barred window and crowned her coal-black hair.

An eye appeared in the spyhole. The iron bolts of the door retreated with a clank. Rebane jumped up to lace her boots. Her sense of foreboding intensified as she prepared for an opportunity. She stood legs braced apart for balance and raised her fists.

All I need is one blow to the chin to make him pass out.

Weisser bowed his head in the doorway. Once inside, he straightened into his full height and offered Rebane a hard look. "There's no need to pick a fight, Miss Nordstrom," he said in a matter-of-fact voice. "Stand down and spare yourself from a beating."

But she targeted the next man who stepped in—a menacing, wide-shouldered guard who opened his telescope truncheon. He drew his arm back to smack her, but Rebane evaded the blow using a simple *Systema* move and nudged him. As the guard folded onto the bunk, she delivered a swift hook into his kidney and wrenched the truncheon from his grip. The second guard leaped at her, missing his mark. She slammed the baton on the side of his thigh, numbing the nerve and thus incapacitating his leg. He slumped onto the floor. Guards number three and four bumped into each other in the doorway. They exchanged glances before the bigger one rushed forward.

Weisser's eyes narrowed as he scrutinized Rebane, who backed up until her shoulder blades met the wall. She'd intended to jump over the bed like a panther but instead crash landed on the blankets. The larger guard grabbed her shirt. Rebane cracked his nose by thrusting the base of her palm into his face. He collapsed on the floor, blood gushing into his cupped hands. The next victim got kneed in the stomach several times before Rebane lost hold of the baton.

As the master alarm filled the corridor, a swarm of men toppled her, but she kicked nuts, thighs and shins. She scratched the faces which came near enough and bit into the flesh of a hairy forearm. She didn't let go until a crowd of hands and knees pinned her to the floor and forced her jaws open.

Rebane prepared herself for what would happen next.

At least I did some damage to the bastards. But at what cost?

The first blow landed on her shoulder, watering her eyes. A jackboot stepped on her stomach. Tears were forced out as she squirmed for air. It took mere seconds for her to lose the fight.

"Stop!" she screamed when violent hands tore her clothing and fists pounded her ribs.

A boar of a man sat on her stomach, growling into her ear. Rebane spat at him, which angered him more. Weisser's voice toppled the commotion, but the guards no longer obeyed him. He grabbed the boar by his fatigues and tore him away from Rebane, but the next madman mounted her and banged her head against the cement.

Yells echoed from the walls. Rebane tasted salty copper when the blood oozing from her nose reached her lip. New blows rained on her elbow and thighs. She shielded her head with her arms and curled into a fetal position. The lightning of pain made her whimper like a wounded puppy.

Fight it. If I lose consciousness now, they'll crack my skull.

Someone yanked her head back so hard her spine let out a snap.

"Gook whore, I'll teach you to behave," Boar hissed into her ear.

Weisser called out for the MPs from the guard station. They stomped along the corridor and had to force their way through the mob. Shoving the cursing guards out of the door took some time, and Rebane shouted, "Fuck you, pussies! You lose a fight with a woman."

Boar turned around and tried to get at her. The ginger MP steadied her standing against the wall as his colleagues blocked Boar's entrance into the cell.

"Are you okay, Fräulein?" the carrot asked. But Rebane concentrated on staring at her middle finger, which jutted out of place. Each breath caused a jagged pain in her ribs as the policemen cuffed her wrists behind her back. They half carried half dragged her down the hallway. The faces of prisoners appeared in the Judas hatches which remained open for breakfast service. The prison doors rang as each inmate banged on whatever carried sound. A voice emerged from an open hatch at the end of the row.

"God bless you," Ivanov whispered with a raspy throat.

She turned to ask, "Is Daniil here, as well?" But the MPs dragged her down the stairs. Rebane clung to slim hope.

He is still alive!

The main lobby fell silent when she stumbled into the first floor and folded to vomit on the tiles. Uniformed officers paused in the middle of their duties, and the secretaries stared wide-eyed at her. The crowd parted like water.

Fuck, it hurts.

Each movement of her torso caused agony. They had broken at least one of her ribs. A buzz signaled a door and the MPs applied a controlled grip. They yanked her elbows up behind her back and forced Rebane to bow forward despite a jagged pain in her side. Resisting from this position was impossible. She concentrated on breathing through the pain.

The chilly outside air slapped her awake. The adrenaline in her bloodstream increased her panic. She stood in the prison yard and blinked at the white-hot sun. A swirl of dust broke against the concrete, and a herd of pristine clouds rushed beyond the coils of barbed wire atop the outer walls. Not a sound escaped from the crowd of prisoners who stood in line with lowered heads. Rebane met the eyes of a skeletal man. His gaze mirrored the mute fear of death.

She saw the wooden poles with binding ropes and the bullet-ridden wall. The firing squad became visible as the line of prisoners snaked, ushered by the guards. The sound of the executioners loading their rifles with new clips made a clicking sound.

If only I could see Daniil one last time and share a kiss, I would face death with a light heart.

She comforted herself with that thought. A young Union soldier stood like a slab of stone, a mere teenager staring into the distance. His rifle, an HK417, hung at the end of his limp arm. The wind dived inside Rebane's torn shirt collar and she shivered against her will.

This is it, then. They'll shoot me.

The guards held the door open for Weisser, who strode across the dusty yellow yard. His sand-colored hair ruffled in the wind when he buttoned up his mantel. The major took a seat behind the firing squad and produced a cigarette pack from his pocket. He clicked the golden lighter three times before it gave a live flame. Rebane watched him blow graceful smoke rings toward the baby-blue sky.

Why are you here if you kill me? To watch?

She couldn't believe everything would end here. The line grew and the guards placed three men in denim overalls in front of her. Which was worse—to watch them die or to be the first one shot?

She didn't know.

The condemned stepped forward, and the enemy tied them to the poles. One hooded prisoner had to be carried. His trouser leg revealed an open fracture, but he didn't have the fit physique of Daniil. The guards bound him tight because he couldn't stand on his own. A moan escaped his lips. The grip of pain was too much.

Weisser studied his fingernails while a captain with a face carved from stone yelled, "Prepare to fire!"

The squad lifted their rifles and took aim. Rebane held her breath because she couldn't cover her ears. The skeletal fingers of death closed around her throat.

"Open fire!" As the Union captain's hand slashed the air, a sharp cloud of shots echoed throughout the yard.

Two prisoners remained alive, and the captain had to deliver a coup de grâce with his pistol. Rebane couldn't understand why the execution company were such lousy shots. The distance was a mere ninety feet. Some had fired above the victims' heads. They'd used blindfolds to calm the execution squad, not the victims.

Rebane though she heard the jingle of Siberian reindeer bells.

Nga, the god of death, awaits me.

Rebane took a deep breath. The MPs loosened their grip, and she used the opportunity. She head-butted the guard on her right before spinning toward his mate. Her kick bent his knee joint backward. The sound of his screams echoed in the air when he collapsed. She kicked him between ribs and ran.

Rebane sprinted across the courtyard despite the pain in her lungs. It was as if her feet never touched the ground. She evaded the first man trying to catch her. Making sharp turns on the sand was difficult without using her arms for balance. She gazed over her shoulder to see if anyone was gaining on her and crashed straight into Weisser. It was easy for him to spin her around and get his forearm around her throat. He squeezed her in a chokehold her until she stopped struggling and lost consciousness.

She came to as the ropes tightened around her chest and made her scream. The pole pressed against her back. Dark blood pooled on the sand, and flies buzzed for a drink. One of the enemy men placed a vomit-smelling hood over her head.

"Can't you shoot a woman when you see her face? Fuck you, cowards!" Rebane screamed at the top of her voice.

Heavy steps approached across the sand. A shadow blocked Rebane's sunlight and the hood lifted. It was Weisser.

"As you wish," Weisser said as he towered above her. Rebane refrained from spitting an insult.

Four soldiers in fatigues emerged. The familiar sound as they loaded their ammo made Rebane think about how many times her own rifle had made that sound.

If only I had my rifle now, I'd kill all these bastards.

Weisser checked everyone was ready. Rebane gazed up and squinted at the phosphorus-colored sun which warmed her face. The black barrels stared at her. Rebane envisioned how her chest would explode.

Käreitär, Goddess of the Flame, please let them finish me.

The order broke and explosions deafened her. She cringed, closing her eyes against her will. The airflow of the bullets grazed Rebane's skin and bits of stone flew when the shots smashed into the wall. Something hot wetted her cheeks—tears.

Rebane fell moaning to her knees when the binds were loosened. She touched her groin to make sure she hadn't wet herself. The ground fluctuated beneath as if it were a living thing, a tomb of moldy earth prepared to devour her. She expected the bullet to enter the back of her skull any moment now. Grains of sand crawled beneath her fingernails like bugs.

No sound. No racking of the pistol slide.

She waited on all fours and her sobs made her nose run. As long as she didn't part her eyelids, she clung to the hem of life, unclaimed by neither death nor life. Rebane gathered enough courage to open her eyes and saw Weisser looming above her. He appeared as a shadow against the fire of direct sunlight. She didn't know if he smiled or not. The major yanked her to her feet. Rebane was like a weightless feather to him.

You never intended to kill me.

This was a deliberate mock execution and torture, but Rebane didn't care. She silently thanked Weisser for sparing her life.

4.
Recruitment

Northern Finland, Ten years earlier

Pertti Nordstrom slouched against the kitchen table, his snoring echoing in the cabin. Rebane moved like a ghost because her stepfather slept light despite having enough moonshine in his bloodstream to bring down a bull moose.

She cleared the empty jars without sound, arranging them into neat rows on the shelf. Hungry flames devoured the birchbark after she added wood into the fireplace so he would remain warm. Her cheeks glowed with anticipation when she sneaked over the wailing floorboards. The crackling and popping intensified and sparks raced up the chimney. Rebane tightened the rucksack straps and straightened her back against the weight of her rifle. She trembled with excitement. One last glance goodbye and the chill of the September air greeted her on the porch.

Rainclouds pressed against the cropped fields on both sides of the birch-lined alley. Stars remained weak, and a puddle let out a slurp. No need to light the headlamp because she knew the path along the forest's edge so well that she could navigate it in her sleep. She quieted her rapid breathing by stopping at the intersection. The dog's panting caught up with Rebane before the elkhound pressed against her shin.

She kneeled for a hug. "Go back, Frost," she ordered. "Father needs a hunting pal while I'm gone."

A lick on Rebane's cheek remained moist after Frost obeyed. Her chin fell to her tightened chest when she thought about her stepfather. They had hunted together for sixteen years. When she was too small to walk in the wild forest, he'd carried her on his back. But nothing could make her turn back now.

The aroma of the damp earth surrounded her and the wind sighed. Rebane hadn't said goodbye to Pertti because Dad would have talked her out of the recruiting plan. Guilt swelled in her chest as the boreal owl hushed its call. The lichen and heather retreated softly beneath her hunting boots. Among the fir trees, the mist moved like a living thing, and Rebane's mind returned to the farm. Pertti seldom repaired the cottage or sowed a hidden field. Rebane was all he had left after Khadne, her mother, a Nenets from an indigenous Siberian tribe, had disappeared in the nuclear war.

"Leave it as if it's uninhabited," he'd always said. "That way, nobody will know we exist." Acting as if they didn't exist had helped the duo survive the dangers of the Invisible Zone.

Pertti could place a shot through the eye of a flying bird no matter how drunk he was. He'd taught her to hunt like a wolf and shoot like the forest guerrilla. Darkness held its breath while Rebane sat on the stone and waited for the first light to paint the cliffs golden. A bear skull dangled from the highest branch of the holy pine, and the air here was dark green. Velvet moss covered the round stones, which formed a half-circle.

Rebane placed a jar of her stepfather's best brew and two shining .308 cartridges at the root of the blessed pine. She retreated and bowed her head in prayer.

Where was the bear born?
Where was the beast made?
By the moon,
with the day,
on the shoulders of the Plough
Then lowered on silver chains,
let down on golden cords. [1]

First light licked the naked trunks and the hollow eye sockets of the bear stared at Rebane to offer a warrior's blessing.

****

The grain truck dropped Rebane at the roadside five days after she left home. She found the recruitment office closed at this hour and waited sitting on the frozen pavement, enjoying the crust of her bread. Morning light played on the ice in the harbor, and sleepy silence dwelled between the fishermen's shacks. The market square appeared deserted until peasant girls emerged with their carts and chatter of gossip. They gave her the evil eye. Her alien features and manly garments reminded them of violent times.

Rebane wore Pertti's forest green camouflage with folded trouser legs and wrapped-up sleeves. Her belt sheathed a knife dad had given for her eighteenth birthday. A powerful Sami shaman had blessed the blade. Rebane removed her wolf fur hat, and her braid landed across her shoulder. She stood first in line when the conscripted men gathered on the pavement.

"Go home. Go back to your husband and children," someone yelled.

"Go warm the stove, woman," another one accompanied his harsh words, but she didn't let herself be provoked.

Fuck you.

A hand landed on her shoulder, and a manly voice pronounced in native Russian, "Never mind those idiots."

She turned to face a young soldier with mischief his eyes and self-importance in his smile. He removed his cap and revealed a bush of tangled chestnut hair. The private shook Rebane's hand. "I'm Daniil Kowalski."

"Okay, I believe you. Now let go of me," Rebane hissed.

"Stick with me, and they'll accept you," Daniil boasted. "I'm a master marksman."

Rebane scanned him from tip to toe—broad shoulders and a fit frame. No doubt a success with the peasant girls. A square face who chewed tobacco peeked over Daniil's shoulder. The blonde wore youthful red on his cheeks as he said, "Don't believe a word he says. He's just trying to get laid."

I knew it!

The blonde gave Daniil a rough-handed nudge and the group of friends blasted into coarse laughter. But Rebane wasn't interested in the conscripted men. They had already been accepted into tonight's trainload. She studied her competitors instead—the grey-haired guy was sixty or older and the youngest boy around thirteen. She was the only female volunteer.

When the recruitment officer unlocked the door, Rebane rushed in and the men followed, elbowing each other for prominence. The Russian sergeant limped behind his desk. Rebane strangled her fur hat while he scrutinized the petite woman before him. Furrowed brows and a tight mouth weren't good omens, but she forced her Russian Federation passport toward him. People coughed and tapped on something to signal that the first choice took too long. The shop bulged with sweaty bodies in their winter garments.

"Look, war is no business for young girls," he said, then sighed.

"I'm a hunter. Take me to the range and I'll show you how I shoot…sir." She pursed her lips. Rebane couldn't say that a Finnish forest guerrilla had taught her how to kill.

An arm wrapped around her shoulders and pressed her against a firm body. Daniil was taller than her, and his coarse jaw scratched her cheek. Rebane wanted to slap him but contained her anger.

"Come on, sir. Give the pretty girl a try," Daniil said with a smooch.

An angry murmur arose from the audience. "Waste of time. Go, home, girl."

But something intrigued the sergeant enough to respond, "Okay, then. You come with me," and he darted up. "All others wait outside until we return from the range!"

The granddad spat on the floor while the others objected. Daniil and his posse ushered the men out of the old shop turned conscription office while Rebane admired the posters in the display window. A busty woman held a bayonetted rifle and filled the uniform of the Russian Federation in all the right places. *Victory,* the text proclaimed, and the battlefield smoke dispersed to let a broad-chested man charge toward the viewer.

"That will be us, Дорогая," Daniil whispered, and winked. Rebane didn't reply, but the artwork made her heart swell with patriotism.

The sergeant forgot his heroic limp and strode onward. Daniil tailed Rebane. Whenever she glanced at him, he smiled with the confidence of the young and robust. Outside the village, a patch of snow-covered field housed the makeshift shooting range. The nearest targets seemed three hundred feet away, and the farthest six-hundred and fifty feet—almost inside the forest. The sergeant looked at Rebane, who swallowed her fear.

"Which ones?" she managed to ask as she slung the heavy rifle from its strap.

"The farthest. You said you could hunt." She detected doubt in his voice and clutched the weapon to still the trembling of her hands.

Rebane adjusted the distance turret of the scope, her fingertips numbing fast in the raw wind. Daniil helped the officer to light his makhorka cigarette.

"Are the targets untouched, so you'll know which hits are mine?" she asked the wiry sergeant.

"What do you think?" he snapped back. " Are you going to shoot or what?"

She stuffed bits of wax into her ears. Taking no risks, Rebane sat on the moist ground and crossed her legs. She steadied the weight of the weapon with her left hand, her elbow resting on the soft side of her knee for support. The cardboard targets flapped in the distance as the crosshairs of her scope hovered over them.

"Shoot three times. I expect each one to be a nine or ten," the sergeant's voice sounded from afar as Rebane pushed the lock bolt forward, feeding the first .308 cartridge into the chamber.

Her finger tightened around the trigger as she slowly exhaled. The shot broke with a boom that sent a bullfinch into flight. The stock knocked against her muscle, but she swallowed the pain. Rebane drew the bolt back and the chamber released the smoldering cartridge, followed by a coil of gunpowder smoke. She aimed anew as her pulse echoed in her ears.

It was impossible to see the first hit through the vibrating air in front of the barrel. Rebane didn't know how many clicks to turn the turret and decided to trust the weapon. She had target practiced with great care. Peace filled every corner of her body as she let out a slow breath and glued the crosshairs to the target. The recoil was the same, but she found the mark again and freed the third bullet without pause. Securing the rifle, she rose. Rebane kicked dirt while the officer limped across the field. When he returned, he held the cardboard before her—a single puncture at nine and two bull's eyes.

"And you said you're Russian?" the officer asked.

Rebane reached for her breast pocket and produced a wrinkled Siberian birth certificate. He checked the stamps and flipped through her Russian Federation passport.

"Okay, I believe you," he said as Daniil beamed like the rising sun.

"Look—I want to accept you," the officer continued. "You are an excellent shooter. But you don't know what war is. I don't want the enemy to capture you." The sergeant paused with a swallow and his Adam's apple bobbed. "A young woman, a girl from my unit…she…they…"

Rebane waited for him to continue as the bite of the wind ravaged her, but he just stood there without words. She glanced at Daniil, who yelled, "Come on, sergeant, you've got to let her join. We need shooters like her!"

"Okay. I'll accept you," the officed replied. "You'll get basic training, and the superiors will decide your fate. They can send you to a nursing school anyway."

Daniil closed Rebane into a bear hug, and she tiptoed to whisper into his ear, "A nurse, blah! I want to fight."

"Me too, shorty," he said. "You're coming with the boys and me."

5.
Raven

"Stop," Rebane whispered to the air conditioning and the blast of cold air obliged. The reprieve didn't last long. The buzz started again fifteen minutes later. A softer sound, the hum of the fluorescent lamps in the ceiling, burned bright day and night. She closed her eyes, but nothing could block out the blazing light. A moan escaped Rebane's lips. Her muscles ached from the stress positions and lying on her side had become tortuous. Lack of sleep had worked its stealthy way through her, and doubts filled her mind.

I heard Ivanov's voice three days ago. He must be dead. No sign of Daniil...

The thought of losing Daniil became agonizing.

She folded her shirt for a pillow and the indicator light of the CCTV blinked red. This time she didn't bother to give the camera the finger but rolled over to face the cold wall. The click-click of the boots of the dayshift guards paused outside her cell door but no one entered. She heard men chatter in the corridor until their voices lessened and she returned to her daily stupor.

When she roused, she tried to distract herself from hell she was in. She noticed the walls were littered with I-was-here messages scratched into the paint by unknown prior inhabitants. Rebane read the farewell lines to loved ones.

I will always love you, Svetlana, Olga, Marina, Julija, Viktorija and the occasional *Mary* or *Sarah*. She even found one *Gertrud* who had to be the forgotten sweetheart of a German underground fighter. *God bless you and the boys. We will meet in heaven,* the line said in meticulous lettering.

There is no Heaven. Now you rot, and that's that.

Some prisoners had scribbled addresses of family members in case someone struck a deal with the devil and returned home. Curses in many languages filled the lower tiles. The guards had painted over the words many times, but the scratches remained embedded like hieroglyphs.

Between beatings, the softeners let her be. Weisser did the interrogating personally, and Rebane played the role of *the grey man* as instructed. She held her mental ground but didn't challenge him, either. *The grey man* was a SERE strategy that would buy time. Survive, evade, resist and escape. She resisted, but a way to escape hadn't presented itself.

The evening wove patterns of frost onto the windowpane and a slip of moon hung in the sky. Rebane's eyelids became heavy until she gave in to the sandman. A raven stee-plechased above the fluffy clouds of her mind. The blackcoat lunged toward the hostile ground and curved up inches from the earth. The tips of his glossy wings brushed the sand in the prison yard as he played with death, and her heart skipped a beat.

Rebane became aware that she stood tiptoe on the bunk. If she gripped the bars with both hands, she could peek at the dimming sky. The raven was real as it came into view again.

Such a skill you have!

She leaned her chin against the ledge when the mournful call rang among the walls.

Craa, craa, craa.

A sigh of loneliness escaped her lips.

The messenger from the land of the dead swooshed behind the window and a thickness grew in Rebane's throat. She loved the bird for its feathers, for its brazen flight. Ravens mated for life, and the male showed off his flying skills to impress a female. This bird tugged her heartstrings, for she believed that the raven and the man had shared the same breath since creation. Even old raven couples went through the courtship flight when spring melted the snow. The pair plunged, curled into a ball of obsidian feathers. How both of them knew the exact moment to pull up was a secret known only to the ravens.

One of them had always followed Rebane and Pertti on the hunt. A single raven circled far above their heads and kept in contact with his flock using that same heartbreaking call which now echoed from the prison walls. She wondered how the rifle on her back could mean soft meat from a fresh kill to this highly intelligent bird. The ten-spiked bull had run half a mile after her .308 had punc-tured his lungs. As she'd reached the carcass lying in the open field, Corvus corax had sat on the moose's forehead. The raven had pecked on the animal's glazed eye-balls and studied Rebane with his sheer, bottomless gaze.

Rebane formed ancient words in her mind's language.

How was the blackbird made?
Who raised the raven?

He was born on the coal hill,
Grew in the darkness of the boreal forest,
He was put together from embers,
Molded from burnt wood,
Made from tar sticks. [2]

Now the messenger spirit soared beyond the coils of barbed wire. He claimed victory above the gathering clouds until the sky swallowed him and the last ray of light vanished.

6.
Water

Rebane jolted awake to the drumming of boots. She fell on the floor, still tangled in the blankets. Her nemesis, the guard she'd christened Boar, tased her when the cell door swung open. The current convulsed through her muscles and sent her heart fluttering.

She wanted to beg him to stop, but her teeth clenched together, and she couldn't force a word out.

The guards besieged their victim. Experienced hands rolled her like pastry while her limbs refused to resist. The hood covered her face and transformed the men into fleeting shadows.

Rebane struggled to locate the guards by their voices as she grabbed the nearest by the trouser leg.

"Stop it! I'll tase you again," Boar's voice growled.

Her chest tightened in anticipation of pain, but Boar didn't fulfill his threat. One of the guards grasped her T-shirt, already moist with sweat. Swift, firm handholds cuffed Rebane and attached the chain onto the belt, which they wrapped around her waist. She threw a punch at the nearest silhouette when her arm regained its function, but her punch missed its mark. The men squeezed her between their hard bodies and spun her around. Disoriented, she lost her balance.

Rebane tried kicking when they strapped her feet together and lifted her like a bundle. The lights in the corridor swished by and the hood rustled against her ears. First there was the hiss of the elevator door and then a drop to the lowest floor which turned her stomach into ice.

You're taking me to the torture chamber!

Screaming had no effect. The guards lowered her onto a chair and Rebane smelled Weisser's aftershave amidst the dank air. They lifted the hood and her eyes adjusted to the light the fluorescent tubes cast into the torture chamber. The sight crawled under her skin—zinc buckets and plastic canisters stood on the cement floor, each filled with water. The gurney with straps and the narrow plank over the sawbucks could mean only one thing—*waterboarding*.

Weisser stood behind Rebane like a wall, his hand resting on her shoulder. He bowed closer and his moist sigh remained on her skin. "Talk, and I won't drown you." And for a moment, she yearned to believe him. "I give you my word as an officer," he added, noticing her hesitation. No sign of weakness ever escaped his attention. "To the contrary of what you think, I don't want to make a woman suffer."

Her shoulders bunched. The nasty smile on Boar's face gave Rebane goose-bumps. She looked up and studied Weisser's features to make sure he meant it, but the major's expression remained undecipherable. He stood near enough for her to sense the heat which emanated from her adversary. Their eyes locked, and something in him reminded her of the wall she'd built around herself. Her mask concealed volatile insecurity, but the connection severed as soon as it had formed.

"You leave me no choice, Miss Nordstrom," he said darkly, his cold eyes hooded.

You'll torture me anyway, just to make sure.

"You should take his offer," Boar cut in. "He rarely makes them."

The hose which leaked water onto the gurney hypnotized Rebane and she couldn't look away. Sweat pearls ran down her temples.

"No," her voice choked as she looked at the major again. The war drum beat wild inside her chest. Her vision narrowed into a tunnel and the pockmarked walls seemed to close in.

"You have to speak up. I can't hear you," Weisser said.

"No! Are you deaf?" Rebane turned to scream at him and bounced up.

A nudge from him and she slumped back into the chair. Rebane watched the bull-necked man as he removed his uniform jacket with slow deliberation. He loosened his black tie and rolled up his shirt sleeves to expose hairy forearms. Weisser took off his glasses and cleaned them against his shirt. The shark in his eyes observed Rebane as he stalled. Her shoulders bunched, fists clenched, but she couldn't say what he wanted. A sideward glance from Weisser and Boar stomped across the floor to grab her by the neck.

Together they strapped her on the plank, elevated her feet and lowered the head. The change in gravity packed pressure into her head, offering a foretaste of suffocation. Rebane gasped frantically for air, tensing against the relentless binds. She prayed that by a miracle they wouldn't drown her.

Of course, you will. That's what you do!

Hot tears to burst between her eyelids as the room spun. The third guard put on violent music. The singer roared from the tape recorder, repeating the same words over and over again as the vicious drumbeats melted together.

Tell them you'll talk! Save yourself.

The electric guitar screamed a prolonged agony that echoed from the walls, and a mad pulse raced in Rebane's ears. She needed to pee and pressed her thighs together to lessen the pressure. Blue lightning made the room unbearably bright. The torture chamber faded into darkness and intermittently flooded with pulsating orange. The combination of the disco lights and the screaming was unearthly.

They played a tape of a baby screaming for help which sent the plank vibrating beneath her. The water on the puddles rippled. Rebane met the steely glint in Weisser's eyes as a sudden silence gouged the room.

What's your next move, monster?

The door slammed against the wall and a shadow shuffled past her. The guards carried a man trailed by a cloud of feces and urine. The dried blood on his face appeared black under the fluorescent lamps, and his fingernails had been ripped out. He didn't resist as the guards strapped him onto the gurney. Boar and the third man hooded the prisoner and pulled a towel over his face. The hose bulged as Boar turned the tab and water rushed to fill the fabrics. The skeletal man shook—not like the living shake from cold or fear, but with a tremor of the brain dead. The music assaulted her ears, and Rebane swallowed the taste of bile. She couldn't have cared less for the man. Instead, a single thought filled her head.

Don't you die. They'll do it to me if you die!

As the music paused between the songs, she couldn't escape the gurgling sound of the man suffocating. The water entered his windpipe, and his ravaged shell of a body fought the force of the liquid. White light bleached the room. Rebane turned her head to avoid seeing but couldn't escape the slurps and coughs.

Weisser stood next to her, tall and burly. The lenses of his glasses gleamed, hiding his eyes as he placed the shovel of his hand on her stomach. His mask dropped. His face was devoid of all emotion. The white shirt glowed blue with the flashes of the blacklight. Another second made the cellar pitch black, but Weisser's image had etched onto Rebane's retinas.

You can do whatever you want. I cannot stop you.

The hose dropped like a boa onto her chest, and the water soaked through her uniform. A chair screeched against the floor, but Rebane pressed her eyes shut. Water splashed. The man on the gurney had stopped groaning. Her heart slugged as hands unbuttoned her shirt and lifted her top.

"No, please, no!" Rebane whimpered.

"You can make this stop," hot breath whispered into her ear.

A prodding finger felt her chest for the solar plexus, which would reveal if she attempted to time her breaths to the doses of water. This wasn't the SERE course where the GRU men would never go all the way and drown her. She didn't dare open her eyes when he tightened the strap around her forehead. Rebane ground her teeth and arched her back against the plank on the sawbuck but her frantic struggle only tightened the straps cutting into her skin.

Weisser moved her wet hair aside. "You are a woman. You are weaker than him," he said with a penetrating voice. "Save yourself."

Boar whispered in the background. What Rebane wanted to say was the very thing she couldn't let slip.

"Begin," Weisser sighed.

The music pounded again. A fluffy towel tightened over Rebane's face as the guards pulled down from both sides. She tried to turn her head, but the strap didn't loosen.

At first, they poured small amounts of water which began to seep through the towel. Rebane counted to ten before she had to exhale. A deep inhalation followed. Water rushed into her windpipes, stinging her nose and throat. She spluttered when the burning sensation spread into her chest. Her diaphragm contracted. Vomit climbed her esophagus, but the cloth blocked its route. More water raced in. The wet towel was glued over her eyes, nose, and mouth. Her fingers clawed at the air.

A voice rang through the darkness of the wet cloth. "Alk, u alk," but she didn't recognize the language.

Weisser's voice rang closer. "If you don't talk, we will drown you."

The restraints loosened. Warm hands steadied Rebane into a sitting position as she folded to vomit. The water rushed out with enormous pressure. Weisser had his arm around her and he radiated heat. Rebane gasped for air like a fish out of water. Pressure tightened around her skull.

"That was twenty seconds," he said.

Twenty is nothing! I'm a sissy.

Weisser sat, legs apart. She had vomited on his trousers. He waited for her to say she'd talk, and Rebane used that time to breathe while her teeth clattered from the cold.

"We start again," he said in a smooth voice.

She tried to claw and bite, but they stretched Rebane on the plank and the cuff chain limited her reach. The wet towel clogged every inlet of air. She arched her back against the coarse wood, and her feet drummed against the plank. Darkness crawled on top of her and smothered her with all-consuming weight.

She had lost consciousness again.

"Ten seconds," a bulletin sounded from afar.

She opened her eyes to stop the hand from slapping her cheek—no music, no lightning—only the silence of the tomb. Rebane couldn't sit upright when they unstrapped her. Weisser held her sitting on the plank with his arms around her waist. She let her head tilt against his shoulder to bargain for time. He waited until her agonal reflexes for air ceased and her breathing leveled.

"Look at me, please," he said, peering over his glasses. "I don't know how much more you can take, Miss Nordstrom. Give me something. Anything."

You are afraid I'll die before I talk.

The gurney was empty. The corpse of the prisoner had disappeared.

"You leave me no choice," Weisser said with disappointment in his tone. He had expected a woman to fold faster. His reputation was a stake and it pleased Rebane.

A small victory.

She was too exhausted to resist the tightening binds. Her wet hair stuck to her skin and she couldn't stop her body from shivering, but the towel didn't yet return.

"It's late, sir. We can take care of the bitch," Boar suggested. He burped and returned the empty bottle of whiskey among its companions on the table. The other guard cracked his knuckles, shifting his weight.

Weisser rose and fished a pack of cigarettes from the pocket of his uniform jacket. He leaned against the table, crossing his powerful legs. The guards drained more alcohol. The color of the still water was evident in the major's eyes as he studied Rebane through the veil of coiling smoke. Rebane thanked the Forest Goddess for Weisser's bad habit which allowed her a pause. She wanted to live.

"No. I want to see how long this Siberian bitch lasts," Weisser replied as he adjusted his belt below his plump waist.

He straightened his back and crushed the cigarette into the ashtray. Boar approached her with the towel and sent Rebane fighting anew. The strap buckle chinked against the legs of the sawbuck, but she was helpless as the hose fed rushing water into the fabric. She lost count of seconds and inhaled water.

There was a splash and a ripple as Rebane's body broke the silver surface of the water and then the deep devoured her. She sank until the sunlight slashing the waves couldn't reach her anymore. The smell of wet cement faded and the waves crashing against the shore washed over the distancing screams.

She curled into a ball, letting the black tide close around her. Through the water, a pair of moonstone eyes stared without blinking. A thin woman who wore a funeral veil shadowing her features stood in the stern of a charred boat. She extended a pale hand that water avoided. Rebane grabbed the bristled bones and the creature lifted her with inhuman strength. Without a word, Rebane sat down on the wooden bench. If she didn't know better, she could have sworn the boat… smoldered. The ferrywoman never asked for the pair of coins legends demanded.

All hope is lost. Weisser won.

The single oar made the silent boat glide over the river of death. Rebane looked into the water, her battered face reflecting on the mirror surface. She wanted to ask the woman if she was dead now, but the creature faced the opposite shore where smoke coiled. Rebane didn't dare disrupt the voyage.

The darkness of a thousand nights condensed where a human took form. There was something familiar about the man slowly coming into view.

Daniil?

No. A distant shadow of her lover still wearing his uniform. His shoulders were hunched, and his face remained in the dark. Rebane stood up and the boat tilted.

"Stop!" An order sliced the water from afar. The boat met the obsidian sand and Rebane rushed to the bow. She extended her hand to feel Daniil's touch as light as the feathers of the raven. He floated forward to embrace Rebane, but his fingers slipped away as violent hands pulled her back. The weight of repeated pushes compressed her ribcage, but she resisted the urge to breathe as the earth shook beneath her.

An earthquake?

But it wasn't the weight of the earth. It was Weisser who pressed hard on her chest many times. He blew air into her mouth and forced her to breathe.

No!

He pounded her stomach with his fists and compelled her to vomit the water which Rebane needed to hold onto in order to stay dead.

Rebane lay on the floor as she opened her eyes. She smelled the moldy cement as Weisser kneeled beside her. She pushed him off with all her strength and drew her arm back. Rebane's fist smacked below his left eye. He lost balance and fell back. His glasses ended up on the floor with a broken lens.

"Fuck you!" she screamed.

7.
Escape

The next interrogation stretched on late into the night. Rebane slumped in her chair in too much pain to do anything else.

Let me go back to my cell and sleep, you bastards.

The paperclip Weisser bent snapped in half. He clasped his hands together on the desk and ordered, "Strip."

Rebane studied his expression, striving to determine if he meant it.

He stared at her through his glasses and repeated, "Strip."

A sensible POW would take off her clothes and be done with it. Two men stood guard outside the door, and if Weisser called, they would come in and beat the crap out her.

Again.

She shifted her weight, unable to decide.

The major moved surprisingly fast for his size. He shook Rebane by the collar like a feral dog trashes its prey. He tossed about her slight one hundred-and-five-pound body with ease, causing shooting pain that made her fight to remain conscious. Her knee kick was a halfway effort, which he blocked by closing his thighs. Her feet flung into the air when he lifted her by the throat and smashed her against the wall.

Rebane yanked him by the tie and continued to pull on the slippery fabric while his fingers tightened around her throat. She resisted, her feet banging against the wall. Sweat trickled down her brow as the pain grew intense, her blood cells screaming for oxygen. As a last resort, Rebane's nails peeled his skin above the hard collar, causing Weisser to grunt in pain.

He didn't loosen his hold one bit, not even when his own blood stained his starched shirt.

She wheezed for air, looking into the strangely unmarked face. The room spun. She knew the major would kill her and never think twice about it. The animal prowess of his stare...

You're the last thing I will see in this world.

The commotion alarmed the guards, who streamed in. Weisser dropped her suddenly, eliciting a grunt as she landed on the hard floor. A metal-enforced boot hit its mark—her kidney. The pain paralyzed Rebane's back. Telescope batons bombarded her legs and arms as she curled into a ball. Boar delivered most of the blows, and the fight went out of her with wounded cries. Boar looked pleased with himself for showing the bitch her place.

She ended up standing at attention with a profuse nosebleed and a loose molar, wearing nothing but her regular Russian army issue underwear. Pale as smoke with a swollen tongue and bruises that encircled her neck, she struggled to swallow her bloody spittle. It amazed her that the major hadn't crushed her larynx.

"Consider yourself lucky," Weisser said as he laid out her torn uniform. "We usually strip our prisoners naked."

His words hit her as hard as one of their batons. Rebane flinched.

There's nothing to find, you sadistic monster. You just want to humiliate me.

It was a show of power, not an actual search for hidden personal items. The guards had taken all her possessions on the first day, and cell searches happened twice a week on her block. Rebane lowered her head and allowed her tangled hair to cover her eyes. She folded her arms against her small breasts.

Weisser threw the clothes at her, and she got dressed—faster than ever before. She fumbled with the zipper and hissed every time the pain in her back tugged at her. That's when she saw the face of the older guard whose name tag spelled HOLGER. He stood in front of the door. His nostrils flared, and he held his elbows wide from his body. Holger's right hand rested on the butt of his service arm and the holster strap flapped open. Red dots spread on his cheeks, and his head jerked as if he wanted to move but his body wouldn't follow.

It took Rebane a moment to understand that Holger didn't approve of what took place here.

*****

Memorizing the guards' rounds became a way to keep the hope of escape alive.

Daniil and Ivanov must have perished. I would have seen or heard something if they were still here.

She listened, counting the shots echoing at the break of each dawn, but all she saw was a piece of sky. The raven circled high above the fortress each evening honoring the dead.

The spirit of Daniil. And I'm the last man standing.

The graveyard shift comprised of older men who didn't mind the eerie silence which dwelled in the corridors during the hour of the wolf. Rebane rehearsed her escape inside the privacy of her head. What ifs became a way to endure the sleep deprivation and the stress positions...the meat grinder of ceaseless interrogations where her only weapon was doing *the grey man*.

It happens to everyone, the voice of captain Petrov, her SERE drill instructor, echoed in her thoughts. *Eventually, they'll wear all of you down.*

"Not you," Daniil had turned to whisper in Rebane's ear. "They'll never break you." She had elbowed him to shut up because she'd wanted to hear what Petrov had to say.

Be ready for a human error. It's your only chance. Make it count.

But if she failed to reach the grounds beyond the walls, the guards could cripple or kill her. No prisoner had ever survived an escape attempt from this facility. Rebane had learned this by eavesdropping on the nightshift guards. She spoke fluent German and Weisser forbade talk around her. The guards froze at the sight of the major as if they were soldiers who couldn't force their limbs to act before enemy tanks mowed them down. But during the creepy hours before sunrise, they sometimes ignored the monster's orders.

Don't fail.

Rebane recognized Holger by his shuffling gait and the jingle of his keys. He didn't open the Judas hatch before his keys scraped the lock. Rebane expected a second soldier to shadow him, but Holger came in alone. He wore wrinkled trousers from a slow night spent looking at the monitors in the guard station. Dark circles surrounded his eyes as Rebane lured him into contact. He didn't ask her to turn for cuffing and the key remained in the lock. He held a cup of hot brown tea in his callused hands. A lemon slice balanced on edge as the smell of vanilla overtook the cell.

A soft soul.

Holger was a thin, wiry man in his fifties, not quite filling out his black uniform as he stood in front of her bunk. He smiled, but Rebane didn't dare change her expression. A flutter spread inside her chest. Her eyes glossed over. The gap between the door and the frame widened.

Rebane feared the door would hit the wall and wake him from his trance, but Holger just changed handholds. The tea transferred its heat to the mug and burned his fingers. Inside her mind, she curled like a snake.

"I thought you'd want some tea. It's cold in here," Holger said, his voice no higher than a whisper. Did he think the CCTV above the door wouldn't record his severe offense if he kept his voice down?

Rebane bared her teeth to imitate a smile. A thunderstorm rumbled inside her head when she took the mug from him. She thought of throwing the hot beverage in his face.

No. Get him closer.

Instead, she folded forward and grimaced in pain. She used a heavy Russian emphasis on her German. "My rib hurts. Boar broke it. Please, you are a kind man. I can tell. I need some painkillers."

Holger shuffled his feet in confusion. He gazed over his shoulder and saw the open door. Then he did something which Weisser had strictly forbidden—he turned his back on her.

Now!

Rebane let the mug chink against the floor when she jumped. She tackled

Holger with her arms crossed and her elbows directed at the root of his skull. His face met the iron door as he lost balance. A crushing sound signaled a broken nose as Holger stumbled on his knees. Blood gushed into his cupped palms and down his uniform shirt.

Rebane snatched the telescope baton from his belt ring and extended the weapon with a sharp hit. She tried to open the pistol holster which housed his 9mm sidearm but failed. The guards used holsters that protected their guns from being snatched by the inmates.

Dammit!

Sweat trickled down her neck.

Holger screamed for help. Rebane smacked his temple with the steel baton. She knew she'd broken his eye socket and cheekbone with that much power. Towering above him, she forced the holster hood down against the stiff safety springs. She jerked the hood shroud forward but the flap didn't open.

Fuck!

The eye of the camera recorded every second she wasted, but there was no alarm yet. Rebane paused to peek into the corridor and took Holger's keyring from the lock. She shoved his feet inside and jacked the ID card from around his neck. Holger lay on his side gagging. She held the baton in front of his face.

"Open your eyes," she hissed. "Don't resist or I'll hit you again. Do you understand?"

He nodded with terror in his gaze.

Holger let her roll him on his back. She took his gear belt and wrapped it around her waist. The holster released the Sig Sauer when she repeated the moves from the correct angle. She opened the clip and counted the rounds. Disappointment shrouded her—there were only ten bullets.

Not enough to break through a shootout.

Rebane racked the slide, feeding the first bullet into the chamber. She slipped out and closed the cell door. The camera on the wall zoomed in on her when Rebane ran around the corner. The clock on the wall beeped 5:30am.

I don't have enough time!

She knew the master alarm would go off the second a guard glanced at the images of Holger squirming on the floor of cell number three-zero-three.

If Holger screams for help— I'm dead.

The morning patrol could ascend the third floor at any minute. For all she knew, she could be running toward them. Rebane held the Sig at the end of her extended arms, the barrel facing the floor and her index finger resting against the trigger guard.

Don't shoot unless you have to. Save your bullets.

She sprinted along the hallway curve and trailed the aluminum ventilation tubes until they dove inside the roof. Written on the door to the right, the sign read *Compartment 3E.* The next doors along the corridor were *3D* and *3C.* Rebane didn't exercise in the yard and she never ate in the mess hall with other inmates. She didn't know which way to go.

The lobby has to be on the first floor. Stairs—I need stairs.

She drew Holger's ID card through the card reader beside *3B*, but the light atop the console stayed red. She yanked the iron bar welded to the door, but it didn't budge.

Fuck! They've disabled the card.

She couldn't return to her cell, either. Her breath jammed in her windpipes, and the baton fell on the floor with a chink. She cursed and picked it up as the corridor blurred. Sweat ran down her back. A massive green door loomed at the far end of the third-floor corridor. Rebane wiped her brow with her sleeve and focused on the sign.

EXIT. MAIN LOBBY.

She drew the ID card through the reader twice, but the console buzzed an angry red. A commanding voice erupted from the speaker next to the CCTV. "Stop right there. Place the weapons on the floor. Kneel and raise your hands above your head."

She tried once more, and the lock released a beep as the door slid aside. An ear-splitting alarm sounded as she reached the staircase in two nervous leaps and looked over the railing. The lobby was two floors below. Rebane rushed down the stairs and tried not to trip as the steel baton clattered against the metal rail. The booming echo of shots accompanied her onto the first-floor landing but she never looked back.

Rebane zigzagged between the round metal tables in the lobby. The control room stood atop a concrete ledge. Behind the bulletproof window, the guards stared at her and gestured wildly. One of them picked up the loudspeaker microphone and the buzzer crackled on the wall, but he didn't know what to say. Her grip tightened on the handle of the Sig and her hair glued itself on her cheeks.

A turnstile gate positioned in front of the main door led to the parking lot. The two military policemen who guarded the checkpoint stiffened at the sight of her pistol. They drew their weapons and assumed tactical stances while retreating with flexed knees.

That's right, boys. Retreat!

She hopped over the turnstile and darted toward the exit. The main door didn't have a card console and none of Holger's keys fit in the lock. The bunch dropped from her trembling hands. She yanked the handlebar in vain. Tears streamed down Rebane's cheeks when she kicked the door. Multiple layers of green safety glass on the window let her see the main gate and the broad road. The windowpane fogged from her breathing, and her moist hand left a print on the glass. Another checkpoint with machine guns, soldiers, heaps of sandbags and war dogs stood at the end of the tarmac. She pressed her forehead against the cold window.

Okay, then, I won't get out.

Heavy boots stomped behind her. The knot in her stomach tightened when she turned to face the lobby. The MPs had disappeared, but a swarm of guards wearing riot gear advanced from both flanks. With their barrels aimed at her and the red dots from their laser sights crisscrossing her chest, Rebane knew her single 9mm had no say against the automatic assault rifles.

The man behind the megaphone found its voice and blasted, "Don't kill her. We need her alive. I repeat—alive."

The weight of the pistol assured Rebane that there was only one way out. She let go of the baton and placed the barrel under her chin. Her finger traced the outline of the trigger as she pressed her back against the door and closed her eyes.

Do it. Make it end here. No more torture.

Rebane remained frozen in her suicide pose while the wind threw sand against the safety glass. The tactical fabric of the riot squad ruffled as they moved. She clutched the gun and not a pin dropped in the lobby.

"If you surrender now, I promise there will be no retribution," the dark voice said.

Weisser walked across the lobby, his hand signaling the riot team to wait.

Rebane desperately wanted to believe him.

8.
Defeat

Snowflakes stung Rebane's skin like darts when she stepped onto the parking lot between the guards. The bitter breeze slapped her face, but she enjoyed her moment of fresh air. An unpleasant acquaintance she had named Blondie for his ashy hair ushered her into the van.

"Don't you get any ideas," Boar warned when he shackled her hands to the metal bar and sat next to her. The bench creaked under his weight.

Blondie fixed Rebane with his stare and the barrel of his rifle. The driver mounted the cabin. A loud cough resounded from the van when he cranked the engine. Through a barred window, Rebane watched the closing of the prison gates and wondered about their destination. She tried to read Boar's face, but he turned away. He scratched the pink fold of fat above his collar—a pig's neck. Blondie drummed the butt of his rifle with bony fingers.

This can't be good.

The soldiers at the checkpoint huddled in the foul weather. Even the muscular war dogs sought shelter from the blizzard and cowered next to their handlers. The boom lifted and the wind-beaten land beyond the prison spread out before them. The van's tires slipped and the driver responded by shifting gears and revving the engine. Black ice gave the tarmac an evil glistening.

"Where are you taking me?" she asked no one in particular.

Blondie's high cheekbones framed an unfriendly face. Boar produced a metal flask from his coat pocket, and his Adam's apple bobbed when he swallowed mouthfuls of foul-smelling whiskey.

"I almost feel sorry for the bitch," Boar said.

"Good riddance," Blondie snapped and spat a lump of chewed tobacco on the floor.

The van rocked in silence, and the clouds marched above the silhouette of an unmistakable city.

New Berlin. Why take me there?

That morning the guards had told her to clean herself using the sink and to wear the civilian clothes stacked on her bed. Always a soldier, Rebane did as trained. She used little water and a towel to remove the filth from her body, relishing the cleanliness. Rebane recognized the simple attire—a knee-length tunic made of wartime cotton, the trousers distributed to the citizens of lower classes for the winter months, and the flat utilitarian shoes which took Union females places. But the makeup had nothing to do with the masses and came from the refined psychopath Weisser.

But what for?

The evil omen curled into a knot in her stomach, but Rebane couldn't resist the temptation. With careful movements, she placed the compact powder on her palm and opened the shimmering lid. When her finger brushed over the sparkling dust, it released a smell of vanilla and roses—a *luxury item for a real woman.* Rebane remembered The Container City, where black market dealers sold anything from dirty nukes to lipstick. The nomads of the Invisible Zone bought without questions asked or exchanged their daughters for valuable goods.

This powder is more expensive than my life.

A reflection of her slanted eyes stared back from the miniature mirror. Applying the fine powder wiped out a bruise below her eye as if the injury had never happened. The knot of fear in her gut loosened.

Another strange detail was the lip gloss—like stardust combined with sunset. Her chapped lips enjoyed the nourishment as she posed for the mirror. In a half-dark spot, she could pass for a brunette New Berlin girl. She pocketed the items for future trans-actions and slipped into the winter coat. When steps approached along the corridor, she turned to say goodbye to her uniform. Her fingers lingered on the emblem of the Russian Federation on her sleeve patch. Rebane folded her torn fatigues with military precision. Her brows knitted, and a shadow darkened her mind.

Goodbye, my colors of war.

The van staggered to an abrupt halt and Rebane's stomach lurched. Two armed soldiers in fatigues escorted the trio across the courtyard where a stone townhouse devoured them inside. A whirlwind entered, throwing snow across the checkered floor. The guards stomped to get rid of the slush from their boot soles.

Blondie shoved her up the stairs. When they reached the top, they entered the first room on the second floor where Blondie told her to sit. The door closed and the lock clicked. Rebane wiggled her hands. Her fingers tingled with the blood resuming its course, but the cloud of fear stayed with her.

She took in her surroundings. The air lulled warm and heavy. Weisser's black mantel hung on the rack and dripped melted snowflakes on the soft rug. The halo of wealth and power dwelled here. The library at the far end of the enormous space had shelves upon shelves stuffed with leather-backed volumes. The rolling ladders offered access to the highest shelves, lost in the dark near the high ceiling. Plush armchairs huddled in groups around tables, each equipped with a reading lamp and an ashtray. Rebane smelled the cigarette brand Weisser favored.

The devil loves to show off.

From the corner of her eye, Rebane noticed the map on the floor of the library, crafted from tiny pieces of mosaic and laden with excruciating care to detail. She took a deep breath and tried to collect herself.

It can't be!

She rose to study the alien borders of familiar countries. With the room still empty, she gathered her courage and walked nearer. Mother Russia had suffered a drastic shrinkage of areas. The flag of the European Union devoured Poland, Scandinavia, and the Baltic states. Rebane narrowed her eyes, searching for the white patch which would mark The Invisible Zone—but the frozen, irradiated zones had been wiped out and replaced by the ring of yellow stars. They'd called the Zone invisible because you could disappear there. She kneeled and traced what used to be Finland with her finger.

Container City had fallen! It couldn't be true. Mad Dog knew what he was doing.

A key turned in the lock, and Rebane dived for the chair. The soft rug muffled Weisser's footsteps. He came straight toward her and Rebane's reflexes caused her to bounce up.

"Relax, scaredy-cat," he said with a tinge of irony. "I'll remove the cuffs."

The heavyset man lowered himself to Rebane's level. He opened the bracelets and slid the key into his trouser pocket. Weisser wore a grey civilian shirt with black slacks. His wide belt had no holster. He was unarmed, yet Rebane harbored no illusions of beating him in a fight. Guards probably stood in the corridor.

An old trick like the Change of Scenery won't make me talk. How stupid are you?

Weisser produced two glasses and a bottle of vodka from a cabinet. She watched him pour. The last drop sent ripples across the surface. Rebane accepted the glass from him and finished the drink without tasting. The beverage burned in her empty stomach.

I need all the courage I can muster.

Rain lashed against the windows. The snowflakes turned to water, which gathered on the windowsill. The lampposts disappeared into a mist.

But don't let him get you drunk.

She burped loudly and wiped her mouth on a sleeve. Weisser refilled. Warmth spread over Rebane's cheekbones. The vodka diluted her alarm and she removed her overcoat. She looked straight at him, but Weisser shifted into a more comfortable position in his chair and placed another cigarette between his lips.

Stop toying with me and make your move, bastard.

The glow of his cigarette intensified with each inhalation. Rebane tasted her fourth or fifth drink. He didn't object when she refilled her glass. She had lost count and decided to refrain from the next one.

Still, he said nothing.

Velvet curtains cascaded from the ceiling. The dusk died with a blood-red glow above the rooftops, and the evening turned black. Raindrops the size of bullets gathered on the windowsill. The cars driving in the street brightened the misty panes with their headlights. Each sound echoed in the enormous room.

Rebane finally broke the silence. "How long have I been imprisoned?"

He surprised her by answering, "Two months, give or take."

It reminded her of the time a lifetime ago when she'd entered the hotel lobby with Daniil and Ivanov. The pain of remembering as her lover awoke— as tangible as a brand-new wound. But his ghost had lost most human qualities. Now he was a shadow who awaited her across the dark water, a hybrid of man and the soul-bird. Rebane closed her eyes to reclaim some of his features. Her hands pressed into fists on her lap as she struggled to remember the pattern of light and cornflower blue of his eyes when the Karelian sun forced Daniil to squint. The veins crisscrossing on his tanned arms as her fingers traced them . . .

I'll forget you eventually. It has already begun.

A lump rose into her throat. Rebane needed more vodka.

"Pour me another one," she whispered.

Weisser obeyed. This time, he remained towering above her. "You are an excellent soldier," he said in a level tone. "I have interrogated many fighters during my career. You are tougher than the men and surprised me. I didn't think a woman could be so strong."

"Go fuck yourself," she said. Anger coursed through her.

The insult produced a dry smile on his face and he continued to peer at her through his spectacles.

To avoid his stare, Rebane studied the huge oil painting on the wall. It featured a pack of hunting dogs that had cornered a wild boar. *No one has seen a wild boar in two decades.* The mounted hunter raised his spear to strike through the animal's heart. Rebane swallowed.

I'm that cornered beast.

A knock on the door startled her. A young man wearing an apron pushed a trolley over the doorstep, and the smell of grilled beef flooded the room. Weisser gestured for the private to bug off and lock the door. He placed steaks on both plates and covered the baked potatoes with sauce. Rebane stalked the fat, which bubbled on the meat and made her skin twitch. Her mouth filled with saliva. She hated how much she desired to eat.

"Go ahead," Weisser said.

Before he had time to place a napkin on his lap, Rebane had wolfed down the beef without hardly a chew. She ripped the vegetables with her teeth before anyone could snatch the food from her. Whatever he had in mind she would face the music with a full stomach. Prison had made her a lightning fast eater.

A caged animal who devours whatever they toss at her.

"What do you want? What would make you cooperate?" he asked while sawing off civilized bites from his steak. Rebane helped herself to a refill of potatoes until the tray was empty. She wiped her greasy fingers on her napkin and provided the truth. "I want to live."

His eyebrows arched. "A straight answer, for once. Have we moved past the *grey woman?*"

Talking to you is pointless.

Rebane didn't continue. Weisser dabbed the corners of his mouth with his napkin and leaned back in his chair while the rain drummed across the roof.

"Look, any information you have is old news," he stated bluntly. "We use multiple sources. I don't wait around for one prisoner to talk. If I did, we'd have no actionable intelligence." The major dwelled in thought while he took small sips of vodka.

A warning brewed inside Rebane and the food helped her sober up.

"Don't you wonder how we found you?" He tapped a finger on his desk for emphasis. "You crossed the frontlines. You were deep inside Russia. How did we get hold of you?"

She gaped at him.

What the fuck?

Weisser had her full attention.

"We knew exactly where you were because we got a call," he continued, as his eyes bore into hers.

"A call?" Rebane couldn't hide the eagerness vibrating in her tone.

"What if I told you that we have people high up in the GRU?" he asked and paused.

"Everybody claims they have contacts in the GRU. That doesn't make it true," Rebane snapped. Her body tensed.

"Don't you want to hear about it?"

Rebane nodded, and he continued with a shadeless voice. "They kept their promise to notify us when you crossed into the Disputed Zone and broke radio silence. You decided to fight and reduced your numbers to three." He paused to reach for a cigarette pack from the desk. Weisser smiled as he looked at her again, a brief flash of amusement in his gaze. "You made it easy for us." He lit the cigarette and blew smoke rings while his eyes glazed over. "And that's not all. The best part of the plan preceded your capture."

Rebane watched how a shadow slithered on the parquet floor. She froze in her chair. The major rose to walk into the corner, and Rebane noticed the camera standing on a tripod.

How did I miss the camera?

Weisser stopped the tape. He opened the door and ordered the guards to take a break.

"Look, what I have to say must be whispered," Weisser said as he stood in front of her.

Rebane nodded again and he knelt. Weisser put his arms around her. She didn't break loose. She needed to hear him out, although an evil premonition pushed sweat pearls onto her brow.

The warmth of his breath against her ear made her skin crawl. "Think back on the mission, on your crowning moment," he said. "Didn't it all feel too easy, too greased?"

The memory of the Russian SV98 sniper rifle was fresh in her mind. A local preparation team in New Berlin had come up with an ingenious hiding place for the murder weapon. They'd even painted the sniper gun to match the exterior of the old bell tower. Rebane had rested the barrel against the wooden railing on the top floor. Everything was coated in bird droppings, and she hadn't wanted to soil her getaway dress. Pigeons had launched into a flight when Daniil opened the hatch. A member of the resistance had sawed the hole during a covert renovation just before the Union President's speech.

Daniil's voice entered her ear. "Wind speed minus two, distance two hundred fifty meters. Correction minus one, ballistic curvature…"

Rebane had blinked to focus on the crosshairs of her scope. A grey-haired gentleman was ranting into microphones. The massive speakers had transmitted his voice across the stadium, which was flooded with people. The general's face had displayed pre-rehearsed emotional turmoil as he'd demanded great sacrifice from the Union citizens. He'd paused for the applause, and Rebane had sensed something was wrong.

I hadn›t been paranoid.

The setting had made her hands sweat—the speaker stood exposed, and the line of fire was straight. There had been no bulletproof screens and no human shields. She'd wiped her brow, and her heart had accelerated. Rebane's GRU handler had people among the Union inner circle, and they wanted this man dead as much as the Russians did, but . . .

"What are you waiting for? Minus two minutes." Daniil's voice had grown alarmed as she stalled. "Reb, shoot him!"

The general had taken a sip of water. She'd squeezed the trigger and allowed a muffled thud to escape from the silencer. The man had slumped and the body-guards had fled the scene while the crowd had roared in panic. People had stomped over one another and Rebane had forgotten to shoot again.

A sniper never forgets to fire again. To make sure.

Daniil had tried to yank her up but Rebane had resisted. She'd gazed through the scope anew. The general had a dot of blood on his forehead—the entry wound. The back of his skull had exploded, and fragments of bone and lumps of brain soiled the red carpet. The president had a surprised look on his face, and Daniil had to rip Rebane up.

Even the weather had been too damned perfect!

She tried to push Weisser away, but he squeezed her into himself, reeking of cigarettes and aftershave. Dread grew in her chest as he whispered, "We arranged everything. It took two years of planning. The senile imbecile wanted to cut intelligence funding and use diplomacy." He squeezed harder and Rebane had trouble breathing. "That old fart would have ended the war. We had to get rid of him."

Her heart a drumroll against her ribs, she screamed, "I don't want to hear this!"

"Listen, I asked for a specialist. But you—I never believed it could be some-one like you—a beautiful young woman."

When she struggled, he grabbed her hair to hold her still before he contin-ued. "I'll bet you walked through all the checkpoints wearing that figure-hugging dress, the hat and all. Every man stared at your legs, your breasts. Each fantasized what it would be like to fuck you. And you just climbed that tower. You finished the old man with a single bullet right in front of his followers."

"I don't believe you!" Rebane shouted.

"I saw you with your spotter, Kowalski, the wounded one," Weisser hissed against her skin. "I sat among the general's closest friends in parade uniform."

He cupped her face between his powerful hands and forced her to look at him. The two enemies stared at each other.

"Listen, I want you to hear all of it. I had to make the plot believable. Even the best-laid plans sometimes backfire, as you well know." Weisser's voice grew. He was enjoying this moment of victory. "I needed your group to verify that the Russians did it. I mean verify with proper rapport and protocol, and confession under torture."

"Why the hell are you telling me this?" Hot tears escaped between her eyelids.

"In a way, you have been working for me during the whole operation. I'm your handler's handler." His voice took on a bullying note.

Rebane balled her hand into a fist, but he wrenched her arms behind her back.

"Fuck you, fat pig! You tortured me for nothing," she spat. "You killed Daniil and Ivanov—he died for nothing!"

He squeezed her wrists until her bones crackled, and she screamed for him to stop.

"Look, you don't have to confess to anything," Weisser said. "In exchange, I want you to play along when I start the camera again. Do you understand?" And he let go of her.

He rose and smoothed the front of his shirt. Rebane couldn't stop the bitter tears of defeat. The buildings on the opposite bank of the street smudged into dis-tant mountains of concrete as she sobbed. The noises of traffic died.

"Rebane! Just say, 'Yes, sir,' for the record," he commanded. Weisser stood in the corner with his hand atop the camera. The red light lit, and the tape rolled again.

"So, we agree that second lieutenant Daniil Kowalski did the shooting, and your role was merely auxiliary?" The major asked with a formal tone.

Rebane said nothing.

How can I escape the spider's web? The more I struggle, the tighter it binds.

"It's time to reply, Miss Nordstrom," he said.

She stirred as Weisser's hand clamped on her shoulder, and he bowed to whisper into her ear, "Comply, and I'll let you go."

He returned to his post by the camera and waited. Rebane faced him and nodded.

"Was that a yes, Second Lieutenant Nordstrom?" You must state your answer audibly."

"Yes! You fucking monster. That's a yes, sir," she screamed.

Weisser produced a document from the desk drawer, his voice carrying the impersonal shade of a military tribunal. "As your role in the terrorist act was minor, and because you are a woman, we have decided to spare your life. In exchange for avoiding the death penalty, we require you to apply your full services to the European Union Military Intelligence."

Even if he enjoyed her humiliation, it didn't show on the major's jowly face. His eyes glinted gunmetal grey as he positioned the glasses down his nose. "Know that you have received extraordinary providence. If you decide to decline at this point, you will be escorted outside and shot immediately. How do you reply?"

"Can I think before I answer?" Rebane asked.

Time. I need more time.

"In my opinion, you've already had too much time to think."

She wiped her tears onto the sleeve of her tunic and straightened her back. "What do you want me to do?"

He glanced at his watch and stared at her, expressionless. "We want you to call out your old contact in Riga and request a meeting. Tell him you want to come in. We will arrange everything to look as if you escaped on your own. You will deliver a message of our choice based on some carefully selected documents…" The major waited for her reply.

"Okay," she said, but her voice didn't convince anyone. Rebane joined her hands on her lap because she couldn't stop them from trembling.

"Put some effort into the act, the way you have displayed your theatrical abilities in wasting my time for two months." His tongue visited his lips. "You're a clever bitch. Don't plan any detours or evasive actions. Don't use any of the *I've been compromised* codes. We know them all."

The spelling error, number three . . . how could you know unless . . . you speak the truth.

Weisser's stare turned into ice. He loomed in front of her like a mountain. "One slip, Miss Nordstrom, and our agreement is void."

Rebane looked straight at him. "I won't. . . I wouldn't. . ." She hated the stammer and pursed her lips.

Stop crawling in front of him, you maggot!

"You know I'll come after you, don't you?" Weisser leaned closer with his hands on the armrests of her chair. "I can see the thought forming in your pretty little head right now. You'll come clean to the GRU and tell them how I tricked you."

Rebane tried to push him off as rage flamed inside her, but Weisser held his ground. She didn't have to look at him to see the victory written on his face. His stance revealed all. Rebane felt herself shrink until there was nothing left.

The interrogation room is an extension of the battlefield, and you beat me to the ground. I failed—we failed.

He lit another cigarette and looked at her through the smoke. "Rebane, look at me, please," he said in a gentler tone, "and listen carefully."

She swallowed the taste of bile and gazed at him.

Play along.

"If you double cross me, you'll personally offend me. If you run, I'll hunt you down. What has happened to you in here, it's nothing compared to the moment when you sit on that very chair again. Do you understand?"

She swallowed the *yes* forming on her lips.

"I'll take you apart, piece by piece, and make sure you feel every cut," he said. Weisser's index finger traced the route of the blade across the smoky air.

The room spun. Rebane knew the monster meant what he said, and the meat, the vodka, tried to climb up her throat.

"You are required to survive the GRU interrogations. I need you to earn their trust, to pass back information." He adjusted his belt. "Put the charm gear on. I'm sure you know what I mean."

She watched him open a folder which carried the nuclear warning sign and the top-secret stamp. He gestured at her with the file.

"This paper proves beyond a reasonable doubt that we have learned to manufacture nuclear missiles again. Not that analogic junk your people put together, but digital, with satellite guiding systems, the works. Removed are all the juicy details, of course," the major explained, "I have written a cover story for you. We need to explain how you got your dirty Russkie hands on this kind of information. Anyway, their curiosity will exceed their caution."

The file is a hoax.

But Rebane had no way to verify it, and she buried her face in her hands. The smoke of another cigarette clouded the room. He chain-smoked. A branch scraped against the glass pane.

Weisser emptied another glass of vodka and slapped the file against the desk to recapture her attention. "Listen, you uneducated bitch. I'll give you a lesson in history. When the U.S. and the Russian federation nuked themselves into oblivion, we seized our chance of greatness. "

«You sure love the sound of your own voice," she muttered to herself, but he heard.

A shadow crossed Weisser's face, and for a moment, Rebane though he would jump at her. The major controlled himself for the most part, but his growl betrayed him. "I want you to scare the Russians out of their Cossack uniforms. They fear our nukes. They will sign the peace treaty on any terms. Convince them to give up land. Do you hear me, Rebane?"

Her muscles twitched under her skin.

I make an undesirable dangle—a lousy bait.

The GRU's defensive counterintelligence unit filters all POWs returning from captivity. Expert men stalk the rendezvous point. Six or eight do surveillance. They will surround, handcuff and strip me to prevent suicide. With the best of odds, I'll face more grueling torture . . .

She thought of pleading to Weisser, of bargaining, but convinced herself to remain silent.

"Just fill my glass . . .please," she whispered raggedly.

9.
Dangle

"Wake up. I need you standing."

"*Ублюдок*!" she spat at him.

Weisser understood the meaning of the insult but didn't reply. He wrangled the cuffs onto her wrists and tightened the bracelets.

Boar and Blondie stormed in. Boar's hunched posture signaled an attack, and Rebane backed up, but there was no escape from the room. Blondie revealed his teeth as if he wanted to smile. He stared at her chest rather than Rebane's eyes.

Sober up! I've got to fight back.

Grizzly attempted to punch Rebane's stomach. She turned sideways and moved away until her back met the wall. She tried slipping behind the desk, but Blondie got ahold of her hair. He yanked her head left and right. Rebane pressed on her scalp with her cuffed hands to stop the pain, which enabled Boar to tackle her with full force.

"Pin her down on the desk. Hold her tight," Weisser ordered. "She knows how to throw a punch."

The guards slammed her back against the desk and stretched her over the mahogany surface. They forced her hands above her head. The position was impossible to defend. One look at Weisser and she knew what would happen next.

No, not this.

Weisser was all over her in seconds. He attempted to fit between her legs. The major ripped her cotton tunic, and the loose buttons jingled on the hardwood floor. He yanked her pants down, but she blocked him by squeezing her thighs together. Rebane folded her knees, but Weisser was too heavy.

His first blow smashed into her left eye and bashed her head to the side. The office blazed into white light. Bubbles and sparkles danced behind her eyelids. Rebane screamed, but Weisser pressed his hand over her mouth and nose and blocked her air. He forced himself between her thighs. She let her left leg descend and thrust her bony knee between his ribs. He groaned in pain.

Let go, pig!

Weisser drew back his arm, and the second hit landed on her left ear. A dull pain cascaded along her cheekbone and the side of her skull.

Rebane sank her teeth into Weisser's fleshy forearm. She bit through his sleeve until she tasted salty blood. He grabbed a thick tuft of her hair and yanked her head back. One of her cervical vertebrae snapped and shot white-hot pain along her spine. He grabbed her naked breast and squeezed hard enough to leave a bruise.

"No. You don't have to do this," Rebane gasped.

His mouth was against her ear as he hissed, "Shut up, whore and let me in."

He stuffed a strip of cotton into her mouth, and his forearm pressed on her throat. She prayed he wouldn't crush her trachea in his anger. She concentrated on her breathing as he plunged his fingers inside her.

"I'll hurt you if you fight me. Let me fuck you."

Weisser's helpers pressed down on Rebane's arms so violently that she imagined her shoulder bones popping out of their sockets. She tensed her muscles to arrange a last stand of resistance. She couldn't let him succeed, but her fight only angered Weisser more, and he pounded on her exposed ribs until she allowed him to mount her.

Rebane repeatedly begged him to stop but begging never had any effect on men like him. Her pleas fell on deaf ears. She cried because of the humiliation and helplessness.

"I know you like it rough," he said as Rebane let Weisser spread her legs wide open because she couldn't take another hit. He took her breasts into his sweaty hands and sucked hard on her nipple.

"No." She tried once more after she managed to spit out the rag. Rebane arched her back and trashed, but the men didn't let go.

She became paralyzed flesh and closed her eyes against the things which took place in the room. Rebane was bathed in a cold sweat. The snickers of Blondie and Grizzly made her ears ring, or maybe it was the swelling in her brain. She prayed she would die.

"Fuck the bitch hard, sir. She's in desperate need of a big hard cock," Blondie suggested, and Boar supported him with nervous laughter.

The office became silent apart from the major's fast breathing and the brushing of his clothes against her naked skin. The burning pain intensified between her legs as he penetrated and started fucking her in a violent frenzy.

Rebane lay limp because she wanted him to finish—for it all to be over. She faded in and out of consciousness. Every time Rebane came to, she could hear him moaning and feel him pushing himself inside of her. She laid with her spine pressed painfully against the table while he took what he wanted from her. He slowed down before moving faster and ejaculating inside her.

Rebane tried to rise when he ceased rubbing against her, but he didn't yet lift his weight. Weisser's enormous body relaxed, and she couldn't breathe with his carcass on top of her. Slowly, he loosened his grip on her throat and air entered unobstructed into her lungs. Weisser leaned over her once more and smelled her hair. He stroked her cheek, and this was uglier than all the strikes combined.

Rebane turned her head to the side as the guards loosened their hold on her. The green shaded lamp lay in pieces, and she had a passing memory of its sound when it had broken against the floor. Large fluffy flakes gave the New Berlin street a merciful haze. Rebane's insides quivered, and a shake traveled along her stiff legs. Finally, she remembered to close her thighs. She rolled on her side and off the table, slumped on the floor and raised herself on all fours. With mechanical movements, she picked up her scattered clothes and pressed them against her chest.

The little dot on top of the video camera shone dimmed red.

They'd recorded everything!

She forgot what her next plausible move was. The headlights of a speeding car reflected on the ceiling and shadows chased the fleeting glow. An angry honk of a horn echoed between the stone houses as the guards walked out, savoring their revenge on her. She was just a woman, and all women could be humiliated with rape.

Weisser wiped himself clean with a tissue. His semen slithered along her inner thigh and made her gag when she understood there would be consequences. Sobs trapped in her throat.

No. Please, God, no…

He tucked his grey shirt under his leather belt and lit another cigarette. "I knew you'd be a good fuck. I knew it from the beginning," Weisser said with an unfocused smile.

His smell hadn't evaporated from her skin. Rebane rose in a dreamlike state. She saw the dots of ruby-red blood on her thigh when she tugged her slacks up. Her trembling fingers traced the syrupy warmth over her left cheek which was in the process of swelling. The bone around her left eye felt broken. She had trouble looking to left because the swelling pressed against her eyeball.

Fresh blood stained her hand as she touched her hair and her knees buckled. They gave way as she finished crawling into her chair. The floor refused to level out, and the humming in her ears grew louder.

If the Russians find out…

Weisser replied as if he'd guessed her thoughts. "Of course, I can always tell my contacts on the Russian side that you slept with the enemy to save your skin. I can even mail them the tape if you deviate from your expected route. I'm sure the video shows your enjoyment. " He leaned back in his chair, totally at ease.

Rebane wanted to tell him this hadn't been necessary. He didn't have to rape her. But no words left her chapped lips.

He added, "You might want to pull yourself together since you should be on board an eastbound truck in an hour."

Her body was no more than loot of war that could exchange ownership between the winners. A wave of overwhelming shame surged over her. She stared at the soft rug beneath her feet and let the tears roll down her cheeks. For the first time, Rebane didn't know what to do next.

Weisser's gaze became hazy as he stared nowhere in particular. "I'm sorry I have to let you go. I'd like to do that again."

10.
Truck

The guards grabbed Rebane by the armpits and lifted her feet from the floor. She let them drag her across the yard where the wind whistled in the corners. A helicopter hovered above with deafening noise and whipped snow into the air. Its searchlight revealed the outlines of an old truck with a plow welded to the front and armored plates covering the battered sides. Rebane recognized the type of vehicle as what the smugglers used to get across the No Man's Land. This one would take her into the wolf's mouth.

The driver gave the truck gas to keep the machine running against the odds. Boar had to yank the door handle twice before it agreed to open.

"Get inside!" Blondie barked at her.

Rebane stepped on the footboard in a stupor and struggled to climb into the cabin. She yelped in pain every time her ribs compressed against the seat. The driver reached out to help her on board. Blondie wired her cuff chain through the handle of the passenger's side door. Rebane thought of spitting at him.

What's the point? The worst has already happened.

"Come on, close the door," the driver yelled in a Polish accent. "I just heated the cabin!" He bashed a hairy fist on the dashboard and caused the fuel meter indicator to flicker. Blondie handed the smuggler the key to her cuffs. Rebane observed how he slid it into his front trouser pocket. The engine died.

"What a Goddamned piece of junk!" he cursed as Blondie banged the passenger door shut.

The Polish man turned the ignition key again and gave the beast more gas. The seat vibrated under Rebane when the machine let out a hellish clank. The reek of diesel entered the cabin as he accelerated through the retreating gate.

The driver turned towards her. "I'm Pavel."

Rebane didn't reply. She faced her battered reflection from the side window as the heaviness in her stomach grew. The townhouses with lit windows stared down at her like glowing eyes.

Don't let it get to you. Think of escape!

She noted the grease-stained sandwich wrappers and the leaky diesel canister in the cabin. Pavel had folded his lambswool-lined pilot's coat between the seats, and he'd wrapped a woolly muffler around his neck several times. Rebane needed his warm clothes if she was going to run. Most likely, Pavel wouldn't be his real name—not a cryptonym, either. Codenames usually meant something such as *fitness* or *revenge.*

Pavel looked well over forty in the light emanating from passing streetlamps. Deep furrows connected his nose to his jaw, and his jet-black hair had retreated from his temples. His weather-beaten skin told Rebane he had spent his life outdoors. A callus on his index finger revealed the continuous rub against a trigger guard.

An ex-soldier converted by Weisser. Men like you swarm the border areas as mercenaries and smugglers.

He slowed down to cross the cobblestone square. The clean streets and silent shopfronts slumbered in the darkness, unaware of Rebane's plight. The motor's running became smoother as Pavel added speed. They escaped into the countryside, and the gravel road narrowed into a slithering ribbon between the flat-topped hills. A mundane curiousness twinkled in his gaze. Pavel spied her from the corner of his brown eyes. She knew she looked as if a steamroller had run her over. If Weisser had bashed her head any harder, she would be in a coma.

You should have killed me when you had the chance.

"What the hell happened to you, sweetheart?" the smuggler asked in a smoky voice.

Rebane narrowed her eyes and gave him her most sinister look. He adjusted the rearview mirror, which hung by one screw. The sky glowed red between the farmhouses, and dawn seemed only minutes away. He broke just in time for the roadblock which came into view behind the curve. She turned away when the soldiers blinded her with flashlights and barked questions. Pavel produced documents from the glove compartment and answered while Rebane's fingers went to work outside the sphere of light. Her breath became shallow when a loose screw from the door panel rolled onto the floor with a chink. The truck accelerated when the boom lifted and she faced front. Her fingers felt for the next screw which jutted out of place.

Pavel attempted to create a conversation. He had to raise his voice to top the tortured engine, which refused to shift into a higher gear.

"The boys were quite rough with you," he said, stating the obvious.

Rebane had no intention of elaborating on what had happened. "Just fucking shut up and drive!" she huffed and closed another screw inside her fist.

He shook his head. "You should know I won't hesitate to shoot you if you try anything."

"And you think I'd care," she hissed between her teeth, but couldn't bring herself to hate the old war dog who spoke fluent Russian. She noticed the GPS pad mounted on his dashboard.

Why? Does the Union have a satellite?

He offered her a sandwich with thick slices of pork on top. Rebane took it from his extended hand and faked a smile. She had to fold her torso to reach the bread in her cuffed hand. Opening her mouth caused pain but she forced herself to chew with care. She had blood spatter on her tunic and dried blood under her fingernails.

Outside the food production zone, the Union heartland remained barren. Pavel wiped the misty windscreen with his mitten. He leaned forward to take a look at the menacing sky. Daylight had already been smothered by the gathering wall of clouds. Rebane felt the rising humidity in the air which promised rain. Miles forward, the gravel disappeared beneath a white blanket and the wind threw snow toward the windshield.

Rebane slouched. Her jaw ached, and she felt powerless. The voice of her stepfather surged from her subconsciousness. "I used to be a strong man, Reb. Nothing could touch me," he'd said. "But the war...I lost myself after the war."

Pertti hadn't been able to sleep. He'd spent days sitting in the kitchen staring through the window at the fields that spread out around their cabin. He'd believed something lurked in the shadow of the forest and would get him if he let his guard down.

Will I be haunted like you? Stare at the outside world, convinced that Weisser's men are there closing in on me?

Rebane wanted to tell Pertti that she now understood how he felt. She missed his comforting hugs. Bitter resentment filled her chest.

I achieved nothing but pain and death.

Tears rolled down her cheeks, and she used her shoulder to wipe them. Pavel glanced at her but refrained from commenting, for which Rebane was thankful.

I'll return home. I'll find my stepdad and we'll survive together.

The old wipers scraped the windshield. Violent rain smudged the view and turned the snow into watery slush. The spiked tires and the powerful motor kept the old beast on the road, but Pavel's expression intensified as he concentrated on steering. The repetitive squeak of the wipers worsened her headache, and Rebane needed something for the pain. The truck rocked when the big wheels rolled over the bumps on the road.

"There is no road from Gdansk forward. *The Smuggler's Highway* got blown up last week," he said in a thick voice that couldn't conceal his worries. "We must cut through the grassy plateau. They plow only army roads, and we don't want to use any of those."

Headphones dangled at the end of a cord attached to the radio console in the dashboard. The light bulb, the frequency displays, and the tuning dials caught Rebane's attention. The Morse code keypad embellished with Russian letters: КОНТР ПИТ. She had sent coded messages with a similar machine.

A burst emitter.

Intercepting and decoding transmissions without the same model receiver and the GRU cipher codebook was impossible. Rebane and Daniil had used a burst emitter to communicate with *The Home*.

"How long until the rendezvous?" A slight tremble appeared in her voice. Rebane bit her cheek.

Pavel cursed the weather and dug out a cigarette pack from his breast pocket. Rebane caught a glimpse of his sidearm and the long blade sheathed in his belt. The makhorka smoke thickened the air.

"Ten to twelve hours to Riga if we don't get caught," he replied. "I need you to make the call immediately when we get into the transmitting zone."

"A call?" Rebane asked and tried to stop the nervous tapping of her foot.

"You know how to use the burst emitter. You're a spy," he stated." Start engineering your coded message. And be careful—I know what to expect," he ended with a threat as he accelerated into a crevasse. Pain shot through Rebane's spine and she yelped.

"Sorry about that, honey," Pavel apologized without taking his eyes from the road. He dug into his canvas bag and produced a wrinkled sheet of paper and a pencil. He threw the mouse-eared codebook at Rebane.

"Look, I want us to reach our destination without hiccups and get rid of you. That's all." Pavel looked long and hard at her before facing the road again. He added in a warmer tone, "I know what the GRU will do to you and I'm sorry about that, honey."

"You belong to the militia, don't you?" she asked. "What does Weisser use to force you into obedience? Does he have your family?"

He shrugged but didn't answer. Rebane felt the moment the door panel came loose. The handle dropped into her hands and sent her stomach fluttering when the truck tilted.

Pavel made the vehicle crawl over an embankment in second gear. Rebane watched through the side mirror how the tires left deep tracks across the dune of powdered snow. The temperature plummeted fast, and Pavel turned the heat on when their breaths formed frozen clouds. The snowflakes grew and the wind-speed increased into a raging blizzard that bleached the scenery.

What if I don't survive the weather?

She had no idea how Pavel could see where he was heading. He folded out a map and tried to glance at their assumed position. The interior light blinked and died, sending them into darkness. Hidden stones beneath the snow sent jerks through the car's chassis and the map slipped onto the floor.

"I can read the map for you if you remove my cuffs," she suggested when the light returned.

"Well, he said you're a clever bitch. He warned me not to take the cuffs off."

Rebane knew exactly who Pavel meant. She could smell his cologne on her clothes and her stomach sank. Pressing on the door panel with her leg, Rebane held it together. She felt the twisted, sharp end of the window lever and forced herself to concentrate.

Thank you, Fox Spirit, for this noisy piece of shit.

The handle rested firmly inside her hand. She needed a distraction to break the panel—to be free of the door handle. Rebane had no intention of contacting her own side. The safety codes and the intentional errors which signaled danger were known to Ivanov and Daniil—and the cunning enemy.

Pearls of sweat formed on Pavel's upper lip. He took a sip from the flask which he produced from his door compartment. The brown liquid smelled with a sting—cognac. As he drank, the corner of his jaw pulsated with his carotid arteries. Rebane decided not to stare with such homicidal intention.

A gale pushed the massive monster from the rear and jackhammered its sides, almost capsizing the truck. Snow flew in the violent wind, and Pavel gritted his teeth. Rebane knew that if they got stuck, they'd both freeze to death. He used excess speed crossing the dune and lock-braked on the black ice. The truck lost traction and slid sideways into the ditch, tilting in slow motion.

Rebane kicked the door panel around the handle. She gripped the lever and placed her thumbs behind the blunt end while she jumped at him. Plunging the sharp metal into his throat came from her muscle memory. She sat on top of him when the truck capsized.

Rebane yanked Pavel's knife from its sheath. She stabbed the side of his throat and serrated his carotid artery by twisting the blade to the side. In a frenzy, he reached for her face, but she turned away. His arterial blood gushed out in synchronized spurts when she withdrew the knife. A sharp pain yanked her out of the killing frenzy—her palms had slipped onto the blade. A storm coursed through her veins. Rebane mustered all her force to keep him in place while she watched as Pavel convulsed and lost consciousness.

With swift movements, she got dressed in his winter jacket. Rebane needed his jeans, too, but she couldn't manage to strip him in the capsized cabin. She cursed and moaned but had to give up after she located the key to the cuffs from his pocket. She didn't have enough strength to roll him over.

The lightbulb on the burst encoder lit as the other side made contact. Rebane yanked Pavel's pistol from the holster and snatched his map and his bag without checking its contents.

Please, Käreitär, the creator of the Red Fox, let him have a compass.

Rebane grabbed the whiskey when the GRU cipher clerk listed the opening identification numbers. She dashed out into the blizzard and screamed as she fell. The snow swallowed her up to her waist. The icy flakes soaked her hair when Rebane took one step, then another, until she convinced her feet to move. She crawled on all fours to escape the deep dune. The wind threw her bloody hair onto her face.

Get the hell away from the truck—it's your last known location. The devil will come looking for you.

She got caught in the next embankment and fell onto her stomach. Rebane climbed up and forced her thighs to work until the snow leveled out. Now she could run instead of wading through the snow.

Run! You're free.

"FREE!" she screamed, but the blizzard snatched her voice away.

She sprinted into the raging darkness until her lungs refused to take another breath of the freezing air. She hit her thighs to get them moving—to take one more step away from *him*.

Pavel's scarf became wet from her frantic breathing. Sweat pearled on her forehead until Rebane pushed the fur-lined hood down. The wind numbed her earlobes and made her forehead ache. Whiteness merged the ground with the sky until she didn't know which way was up.

You're running in circles and you'll end up back at the truck!

The wind swirled the snow into high pillars, and the gales pushed her back on each step until she agreed to flatten against the hillside. She still shivered, which was a good sign. Breathing became incredibly hard when she tried to crawl again. With her last bit of energy, she clawed inside the white earth toward the inner layers—until she tumbled to the soft bottom. The frozen hand of the Ice Queen wiped her tracks and Rebane smelled the ozone.

She became too exhausted to feel the fear which had driven her this far. Rebane curled inside the dead smuggler's lambskin jacket. She clasped her hands in Pavel's mittens against her chest and drew in her knees. Against all the odds, the fugitive fell asleep, nestling in her snow cave like the arctic fox. The howls of the storm distanced and intense warmth caressed her.

PART II

11.
Fugitive

Sleet turned to ice, clogging the hole Rebane had punctured for air. The ceiling of the cave was lost in darkness. A voice nagged at the back of her mind.

You'll run out of oxygen.

But she was too exhausted to move. She drifted into unconsciousness while the wind screamed outside the shelter, a distant roar of the wounded bear. The gusts conjured a ghost of Rebane's mother—a petite teddy bear in her layered reindeer parka. Rebane mistook the euphoria she felt as the joy of returning home, but her breathing had become shallow. The nest sealed off from the outside world.

Rebane didn't remember much but knew the tribe had named her mom *Khadne*—the blizzard woman— because she was born during a record snowstorm. Her dreams had molded a Nenets woman who chased after her wild fox daughter and closed Rebane into a bear hug. Through the haze of over two decades, she'd watched mother's hands wield the butcher's knife, and from time to time, Khadne had paused to blow on her frozen fingertips. She had the kind of face Rebane had loved to study without end.

Rebane smiled in her sleep. The reindeer bells echoed from afar. Khadne wiped the sleek hair off her face, the same raven-black which had once made Rebane proud of her beauty. Mother sang in words that had lost meaning but made Rebane's heart ache. Khadne's slanted eyes had decreased into lines when she arched her back and released tinkling laughter.

Can I be the descendant of such a celestial being? A Goddess of Wind and Snow.

"Reb, wake up," a manly voice urged. "Get on your feet, sleepyhead, or you'll freeze to death."

Rebane had no willpower left in her aching limbs. She drew her knees against her stomach and let the bliss of heat gather into her core. Powerful paws grabbed her shoulders, but she refused to let go of Khadne and her place by the yurt's sacred fire. A rumbling noise freed the call of the wind, and clumps of ice-crusted snow hit Rebane's face like punches.

Opening her eyes revealed nothing but blackness. She sank her claws into the soft walls and crawled up the slope. But the structure caved in and Rebane fell to the bottom with a thud. The sky dawned above, but another rumble sounded, and the avalanche buried her deeper. The suffocating wetness gathered heavier on top of her. All she could do was whimper until the oppressive whiteness clogged her mouth and nose.

Certain she would die, Rebane felt muscular arms form a lifebelt around her waist. The warmth of a familiar breath brushed her cheek. Sandpaper skin slid softly against her jaw. Rebane's hands fisted in his uniform and air flooded into her lungs with sharp, hungry breaths.

She hung onto Daniil as if she were a drowning person, but his matter thinned and slipped away between her fingers, commanded by forces stronger than love. Without support, she collapsed onto the hillslope with hot tears running down her cheeks. Rebane pressed her hands onto her temples and begged, "Don't go. Daniil, don't leave me!"

But his blurred outline merged into the blazing light. As Rebane crawled on all fours to follow, the rose gold of dawn swallowed him. She buried her face in her hands. Heaves of sobs shook her shoulders until she couldn't breathe without blowing her running nose. The light diminished until pregnant clouds sank lower, their hems wiping the rocks. Straightening herself, Rebane shook her head to clear it.

"Ouch!" The nerve pain traveled below her left eye and ended up as lightning at the root of her molar.

She trailed the outline of her cheek, which was the size of an apple. She squeezed the swelling between her index finger and thumb and wondered if infectious pus would spurt out. Rebane scraped the crust of dried blood off her wounds. Her eyes trailed down and noticed the purple on her wrists. Enough time had passed to make Weisser's handholds visible and to turn the edges of the bruises yellow. She had no intention of studying her blackened sides in the plummeting temperature. Rebane swallowed the tears searching for an outlet.

Get a grip, you idiot! They're onto you by now, and you must decide a heading.

She rose with grunts of agony. The sun hid behind the wall of slab grey. No trees grew here to reveal the time of day by their shadow. Rebane shielded her battered face by lifting the fur-lined hood. She scooped snow by the handfuls and let the crystals melt on her tongue as she calculated her location. Nothingness spread in all directions beneath the castles of clouds towering in the sky. The needle flickered restlessly when she took Pavel's compass from the pocket and she pursed her lips. Rebane rotated around her axis thrice. Finally, the needle settled on magnetic north. She shaded her eyes to find a landmark toward which to head. A winding road, a hilltop—something which would stand out. But pallid nothingness shaped the earth around her and her face tightened.

How far am I from the crime scene? Six miles, tops. Not enough, because the deep snow slowed me down.

She remembered Pavel's bag.

If I dropped it at the bottom of the cave, I'm lost.

A cold sweat broke from Rebane's pores until she felt the weight of the smuggler's bag resting against her buttocks. She found the zipper intact, with the precious survival items dry inside the oil-coated fabric. Rebane placed the thin plate of emergency food on her palm and unwrapped the tin foil. A squiggle of a timestamp argued *Expiration date: 1.10.2037*, eleven years past the due date. Suspicious, she nibbled a piece and tasted the plywood.

War preservatives are eternal, like stones.

Unfolding the map revealed a numbered military grid, an excellent resource, and Rebane reminded herself to correct her compass reading for declination. Pavel's flashlight had swallowed ice-cold water and refused to light, but she saved it for later repair after she found a place to hide.

I can't risk using a light anyway.

A restlessness resurfaced and she ran her finger through her hair. Finding several knots, she soothed herself by disentangling them strand by strand. There wasn't even a rock to duck behind if a black dot hovered above the horizon—a drone, or worse—a military helicopter.

Just one reconnaissance flight and he will find me.

She considered several scenarios while unwrapping the second tin foil. She felt her innate strength return as her blood sugar levels rose. Plan Number One across radioactive Sweden would be the shortest route to Finland but was off-limits if she had any wit. Number Two, aka Norway, was too mountainous to cross on foot, especially without climbing gear. Number Three contained obeying the monster who raped her.

She remembered the hungry eyes of Blondie and Boar on her naked body and bitter stomach acid rose into her mouth.

"Fuck you!" she shouted loud enough to scare herself, but the wind didn't answer.

Rebane wanted to vomit but gulped several mouthfuls of the smuggler's cognac instead.

If I start processing what happened I will shoot myself here.

Pull yourself together, soldier! You must lose the hunters and cry your eyes out later.

She repelled the chilling thought of Weisser and his goons and analyzed her options.

I can convince the GRU in Riga. They'll believe I had no choice.

But Rebane wouldn't trust a prisoner who'd spent two months in the hands of an enemy. Why would the GRU interrogator believe anything she said? If she wanted the Russians to take her in, she should have behaved with Pavel.

Not an option anymore.

Home. I must disappear into the Invisible Zone. Dad will help…if I can convince him to forgive me.

Although Northern Finland seemed the best choice wherein to vanish without a trace, Rebane didn't know where No Man's Land ended, and the front-lines of war started. She remembered the map on Weisser's floor—the Union-conquered Invisible Zone.

I can't walk across the Baltic Sea, not even if it's frozen solid. I'd walk blind into a Union outpost.

She chose to enter Sweden and approach Finland via the wild outback of the north. This meant turning northwest now and crisscrossing through Union ground toward the sea. But the problem of the secret file remained. Rebane fingered the coarse manila cover leaf of the record and traced the nuclear warning sign. She didn't take the cursed file out of the bag.

I must pass this on. What if there's another nuclear war coming? My people deserve a warning if that's the last thing I do on earth.

And Rebane could think of only one person she could trust with such information—a woman in Rostock who belonged to the resistance. Frau Engel knew people who in turn knew other people connected to the GRU. And Engel could pull local strings, buy military-grade gear from guards crazy enough to steal from the Union military base.

I need skis and a quality rifle. And a Geiger meter with a killer battery. That's the bare minimum if I'm mad enough to enter Sweden. One hundred and sixty miles to the target. I'd better move now.

She started at a jogging pace, adding speed after the sting in her side stopped. Rebane could cover twenty miles in one day, but not in her present condition. She ran and walked intermittently and the method worked. A snow bunting startled into flight, and her heart jumped into her throat. The rocky terrain leveled out and she removed the hood as sweat glued the tunic to her back. A bronze mist drifted over the western horizon.

Rebane paused to sniff the wind. She smelled the polar fox before the white fluff of his fur appeared above the ridge. The animal continued padding with a relaxed pace, carrying a ball of white feathers between its jaws. The fox stiffened at the sight of Rebane when she sprang toward him. She waved her hands in the air and hissed between her teeth. The fox's amber eyes locked upon hers, but the animal didn't know how to react.

"Drop it!" she commanded.

He released the dead willow grouse and galloped for his life. The polar fox halted on top of the next ridge, staring at her with bitter accusation in his eyes. His pink tongue hung from his mouth.

Rebane thanked Käreitär for stumbling into her harmless totem animal instead of a pack of wild dogs or worse. She stuffed the willow grouse into Pavel's canvas bag as guilt nagged at her. As she distanced herself from the crime scene, the fox trailed her. He stopped to lick the drops of blood from the snow, a white feather hanging from the corner of his mouth.

"Consider yourself lucky." Rebane turned to speak to the fox. "I could eat you. I have a revolver."

The fox sat on his fluffy behind, swirling his duster tail around his front paws. Cute ears flattened against his head when he scowled at her. Rebane rubbed her earlobe. "Maybe I should let you have a piece?" she muttered to herself. "Considering you're the hunter."

His head tilted as the animal listened. The secret fire in the fox's eyes tried to decide if the human was harmless or dangerous. The animal took two steps toward her, stopped to observe and padded closer. Rebane remembered that to offend your guardian spirit was never a good idea, especially on the run. She bit her lip and kneeled. The smuggler's blade severed the bird's leg without effort and left a delicious chunk of meat dangling from the bone. She threw her offering of truce on the ground and retreated.

The fox snatched the leg with a sly smile on his face. Soon, the animal merged into the white background, gone as if it had never existed. Rebane pulled the scarf over her chin, smiling in secret.

A hell of a camouflage! I'm envious.

At twilight, she mounted the highest hill to get an overview of the terrain. She lay on her stomach as the dwarf birches knotted their branches above her, providing meager camouflage. She let her eyes adapt to the darkness which spread over the plateau like a blanket. A road curved westward at the root of the hill, the tarmac plowed clean. This meant traffic—danger—and she became a ball of angst.

I'll injure myself on the rocky terrain if I run through the night. I must follow the road.

The light of the lessening moon crept over the grounds like quicksilver. Hunger made Rebane's stomach growl like a wolf. She yearned to taste the roasted grouse. She swallowed a mouthful of saliva, but a pillar of smoke would alert anyone within five miles.

I'm so fucking hungry!

Because of permafrost, she couldn't dig the fire underground, either. She pushed the thought of eating into the back of her mind and started descending the slope. Rebane tested each step before putting all her weight on it in the dark, hearing pebbles roll downhill.

Midway down, her gut shrank. She picked up the unmistakable *whop-whop* of helicopter rotors before the searchlights sliced the sky.

Hyperventilating, Rebane dashed uphill and dived under the cover of the birches. She slithered between the rocks, drew the hood over her head and prayed for the crew not to spot her.

The noise became ear-splitting before the potbellied military helicopter hovered over the hill, its skids brushing the treetops. No way the pilot could land here. The airflow bent the birches and whipped up pillars of snow. Stones rolled down the slope. She waited without breathing.

They must see me!

She expected bullets from the machine guns to impale her at any second, but instead, the helicopter turned to propel north. The searchlights combed the dark terrain.

So much for the fucking element of surprise!

Her knees turning to water, Rebane forced herself to rush downhill blind. She landed onto the tarmac with her pulse ringing in her ears.

She ran faster than ever before.

12.
Evasion

They must have night vision—infrared. They will be back in numbers. Weisser wants me alive.

The Sikorsky used a searching spotlight to sweep the ground just south of her position.

Maybe they missed me by a few feet...

Rebane followed the road, making fox loops on both sides in case they employed bloodhounds. She wore a grave face as she thought of the Sikorsky, who'd probably combed the bushland all day for the infamous needle in the haystack—*her*. She knew Union helicopters could carry up to four hundred gallons of fuel. And they'd found her at dusk, just minutes before they would be forced to return to the nearest airbase.

There were risky ways to fool thermal cameras—causing an explosion or fire, but the time window to escape on foot was narrow. If the search party didn't see her, making a fire would be madness. The sky was quiet as the grave. Rebane had an hour or two to get as far away as possible from this location.

Goddammit! I'd give my left arm for an Electromagnetic Pulse gun. The bird would drop dead from the sky.

Further up, she deviated from the tarmac again, only to return a half mile later. Her thighs gave her hell for running to the forest rim and back.

A half-an-hour later, the moon rose like a giant spotlight and the tarmac glittered while she forced her tortured legs to add speed. The rubber-soles of her shoes tapped on the asphalt and her heartbeat echoed in her ears. Walls of white guarded the flanks where the plow had pushed snow into heaps. If she had to dive for cover here, it would take minutes to climb over, and before the trees there was more snow, cursed and knee-deep.

I'll see their headlights if they come along the road. And I'll hear the motors.

The magpies circled above and settled back on the trees. Her feet slipped on the ice. Rebane tensed her muscles to maintain balance, slowing her pace, her fists still clenched.

Don't you fall now! You sprain an ankle and they'll get you.

After circa five miles, she paused to listen for the rotational hum of the helicopter, but only darkness resonated around Rebane. Her breath misted the cold night when she tilted the compass to catch the moonlight, and the dew from her breathing made teardrops on her scarf. The compass needle raced around the orbit and struggled to settle on a choice of degrees. Something was causing interference.

Radiation?

If I have trouble navigating, so will the Sikorsky pilot.

Rebane remembered the offering to the polar fox, its magic in effect by now.

Thank you, Käreitär, Goddess of the Flame and the Foxes.

The pain in her jaw joint reminded her of the blows she'd suffered. Rebane's nose had no feeling when she took off her mitten to pinch it.

Could be the subzero air, or else the nerve ending to my nose is dead. That cursed Weisser...

Anger splashed onto her skin as heat and sweat pushed out from her scalp. She unzipped the coat, letting the subzero air calm her down. The wind cut like a knife, releasing her from the emotional turmoil.

Concentrate on survival. All else is trivial.

Rebane swallowed three mouthfuls of the smuggler's cognac and burped. "What shit! I wish I had a jar of Dad's moonshine."

The cold air chilled her lungs. As she gazed up, Orion's belt punctured the velvet horizon, marking the night's progress. Saiph, the bottom star, shone like a jewel against the Night Goddess's dark skin. Rebane traced the hunter's constellation with her finger and swallowed the thought of Dad's cabin. Orion used to greet her on the southern horizon on winter nights. When Pavel's bag became burdensome, she ran the strap over the left shoulder, evenly adjusting the weight.

The silence sounded impenetrable as she stood in the middle of the road waiting for her strength to return. Firs shuffled in the forest, their branches embracing. The Milky Way ran above her head and the snow reflected the cold light of the North Star, the Big Dipper, the magnificent Sagittarius. A magpie voiced its call and another one echoed an answer.

She ran through the dark silk of the night. The weight of fear rode on Rebane's shoulders, forcing her to run when she no longer felt her legs. The hard terrain hurt her knees with every step. When the rose gold of dawn killed the stars in the east, she searched for a hideout in which to spend the day—a patch of forest, long grass in a field, a hole in the ground...

The first clouds of dawn appeared and dissolved until only Altostratus formations remained. Rebane abandoned the highway for a forest meadow. A dark veil clouded the paling moon and the air was saturated with moisture. The shapes of evergreen conifers moved in the wind, predicting rain.

"Don't get wet. You'll die of hypothermia if you do," Rebane muttered to herself.

She opened her palm to feel if it was raining—*not yet*. She ran a mile or two with her knees no longer able to flex and made one last pair of fox loops. Exposed in daylight, a drone would easily spot her. Rebane entered the forest when sunlight cracked the clouds and bleached the meadow.

Fog rested on the forest floor with her. Moisture gathered on the leather of the jacket and a heaviness settled into her limbs. It started to rain—a drizzle at first, but then droplets drummed the ground with fury. Fir needles sparkled with water when half-dead Rebane crawled under a tree. By now, Pavel's clothes smelled of wet dogs. The musk of decomposing earth mixed with a pine scent. The ground prickled through her trousers but she couldn't have cared less. Numb from the running and delusional from lack of sleep, Rebane lay flat on her back.

But the forest floor soon became too wet to sleep on.

She rose to scan her surroundings. Rebane spotted a half-buried skeleton of a pickup in the field and moved closer. The pallet was full of wet leaves and the hood gaped open. The motor was gone. She peeked in from the passenger's side and met a beady pair of eyes. A mother rat nested in the driver's seat, suckling a litter of pink baby rats. The animal had ripped foam from the cushion and had insulated the nest. Her whiskers moved as she caught a sniff of the intruder. Rebane crawled inside, minding the shards of glass. The rat let her.

Rust stained her hands with every touch of the car's interior. She curled on the passenger seat, wrapping the coat tighter and lifting the dead man's collar. She couched her hands in her pockets for warmth as rain drummed the roof with a sluggish pace. Tossing and turning, she finally settled into a dreamless rest.

She woke when the sun was low in the grey sky. It was late afternoon and the ground had dried. Her stomach lurched for food. Rebane's legs resisted when she crawled out of the window to gather some lichen and moss, knowing she could soak them in melted snow for nourishment. Damp clothes clung to her skin when she stretched and yawned.

"AAH!" She folded from the pain in her jaw. "Don't open your mouth wide, stupid," she reminded herself.

Combing the forest floor revealed frostbitten blueberries and a metal bar suitable for self-defense. The lingonberries were still pale on the underside, but she wolfed them down anyway. Frozen snow had survived the day's warmth under the branches and Rebane melted it in her mouth for hydration. She dipped the moss into the cognac and chewed. Her spirits lifted as her blood sugar rose to normal.

The sun banished the chill, and her hair flapped around her face in the gentle breeze.

"This is nice. You've chosen a great place," Rebane addressed the magpie, which perched on a low branch. A pair of them had followed her through the night, hoping for something to eat. The bird tilted its head, listening. "Thank you for keeping me company," she whispered. The sun touched the tree-tops and the shadows grew long.

I have time to kill before dark.

Within eyesight of the road, she opened the canvas bag to look at the willow grouse. Rebane had drained the blood and removed the bird's entrails earlier. Now she searched for dense ground with a layer of clay and dulled Pavel's knife by digging a hole into the earth. When the roasting grave was deep enough, she gathered round stones and lined the makeshift oven. Bark and dry wood would tend the fire. The army lighter struck a spark but the flames quickly extinguished.

The grass is moist.

She searched anew for a dry tuft. After a few unlucky tries, Rebane stayed on all fours, blowing into the fire from different angles. The smoke devoured the nest of grass and the flames grew. She covered the oven with a shade of branches and leaves to prevent a pillar of smoke from rising to the sky. Rebane sliced the bird while she waited for the stones to heat and the wood to burn into embers. Making a neat package of wet leaves, she laid the meat at the bottom and covered the hole with embers and more firewood.

While the willow grouse roasted in the pit, seasoned with lichen, she walked to observe the scene atop a knoll. Nothing moved on the road. The smoke from the buried fire slithered on its belly like a snake and the wind dispersed the rest. The tranquil forest created a sense of false security.

She swallowed a mouthful of saliva when she thought about tasting the willow grouse. Sitting under a tall fir, she observed a spider hanging from a glittering string. A gale carried the insect to the next offshoot, and the spider straddled back to start a new line from the center. The industrious animal worked to create a precise pattern which all spiders knew by heart.

You know what you're doing although your head is the size of a pin.

To remain sharp until dusk, Rebane studied the declination diagram at the bottom of the military grid map. She corrected her bearing before twilight spread over the land. She walked wearily to the pit like someone wading through water. The wind carried a delicious smell, and nothing stalked in the shadows, but her stomach lurched, and her fear once again rose.

What if I'm pregnant?

She unzipped the lambskin coat to cup her breasts in her hands.

The same size as before.

She didn't feel pregnant, but little time had passed...and few women had been with child since the nuclear war.

I'll rip it out with my bare hands if it comes to that!

A vibration traveled along the road before the noise from the motors grew distinct. The convoy's headlights brushed the twilight forest and made Rebane duck for cover. A scent of diesel stayed in the air long after two army trucks swooshed by. Black motorcycles followed in a scattered formation. Exhaust fumes mixed with the evening air.

Terror pierced her chest. Rebane clutched her pistol.

Pressed flat against the ground, she waited until the noises distanced. As she ran parallel to the road in the cover of the vegetation, a single headlight came into view, far behind the leading group. The driver of the motorcycle stopped at the roadside and switched off the engine. It was a young man in head-to-toe cold weather camouflage. Rebane's heart raced.

He spoke into a walkie-talkie. "I have to take a shit. I'll follow you in a minute."

The other side responded with laughter. "Over and out," the static male voice said.

The trees with their lush lowest branches offered a perfect stalking place. Rebane melted into the shadows and crouched, immobile and tense. The soldier crossed the roadside ditch with one leap, heading straight for the forest. Shoulders bunched, fists clenched, Rebane held her breath. The wind ruffled the leaves and sang between the pines.

She knew what to do. Rebane had ambushed soldiers a thousand times before. *Don't look at me.*

The young man grunted as he opened his belt and fumbled with his zipper, which refused to open. He tapped his feet against the ground as if he would shit himself any second. Rebane squeezed the iron rod in her hands. Without gloves, the surface felt like ice. Rebane stalked the road, but only the single man moved among the vegetation, a mere six feet from her.

You make so much noise! You don't expect anything leaping out at you from the darkness.

He lowered his trousers, and squatted with a fart, the smell hideous. Rebane placed her feet with care, sneaking closer, sure to make no sound as she stepped on the grass and twigs. She raised the bar and froze. Then she swung with all her might, the weight of her body following the trajectory of the iron bar.

Crunch! His skull broke.

The soldier slumped on the ground. He lay on his side, trembling, blood oozing from the head wound and spoiling his winter camo. Rebane loomed above him with the bar raised for a final strike.

"Die," she said coldly.

The soldier's lips moved, but no words came out. His eyes rolled into white, and blood spilled on the grass. Wild-eyed, she bowed to take a closer look.

Should I finish him off?

No, he can't fight back even if he wanted to.

Rebane went to work. She grabbed the man under his armpits and crossed her hands over his chest. Panting and cursing because of his weight, she dragged him toward the forest.

Fucking fat pig! What do they feed you to make you this heavy?

She changed holds and ended up dragging him feet first. But his shirt got tangled to the thorny bushes uphill and Rebane had to give up. A trail of blood and drag marks revealed his location.

She sprinted back onto the road to capsize his motorcycle into the ditch. Leaving the radio chatter on, she covered the vehicle with slush, leaves and twigs.

Rebane swept the drag marks with a branch from a fir tree and returned to harvest his gear.

The man's dead eyes stared into nothingness.

She removed his padded trousers while uttering her most potent curses in Finnish. Just in time because a puddle of urine had escaped his bladder. Rebane yanked the camouflage coat from his carcass. She struggled with the sticky-wet buttons and the zipper, all drenched in blood and brain matter. Even when she threaded his belt twice around her waist and rolled up the sleeves and trouser legs, the padded winterwear of the Union army hung enormous on her. Rebane found a Sig 9mm pistol snugged in a belt holster with two loaded clips, each with twenty bullets. Her face red, she still gasped for breath. Undressing a dead man was hard work.

Binoculars hung by a leather strap around his burly neck, and she cut it with Pavel's knife, too exhausted to lift the guy's head.

His gear is a stroke of unbelievable luck!

Rebane wanted to raid the saddlebags on the bike, but too long a time had already passed. The first stars had already lit in the eastern sky.

His grave remained sloppy, shallow under the trees. Rebane's body overheated from the burial and the excitement of near combat. Wiping a sheen of sweat from her brow, she struggled to calm down.

Locating his body won't take much searching if the convoy turns around.

Rebane unearthed the scorched bird and smothered the fire by stomping on it. She held her breath and listened past her drumming heart.

Nothing.

Just the magpie calling and its mate replying. Beyond hungry, she untied the leaf package and tasted a slice.

"Delicious."

She swallowed most of the grouse before she remembered to save some for the birds. The dying light painted a silhouette of the magpie pair as they rode the top of a birch tree like children in an amusement park. The birds chattered amongst themselves and kept a lookout down the road. Rebane knew the alarm voices magpies used to warn about approaching humans. This pair had already grown familiar with her and the smell of the roast.

Rebane knelt and froze. She held a piece of meat on her open palm. The braver bird spread its black and white wings and the wind lowered him to the ground like a caressing hand. He folded his wings and hopped closer to the human.

"Come here. I won't hurt you," she whispered.

The bird looked at her, still undecided if the meal was worth the risk. Rebane waited until the bird had gathered enough courage to land on her hand. His clawed foot formed a tight hold around her middle finger.

The magpie used his sharp beak with surprising finesse. He turned his head to stare at her with those bottomless eyes but didn't swallow the meat.

Tell Daniil, I miss him, little soul bird.

When she moved, the bird startled into flight. Rebane sprinted down the road, heading for Rostock.

13.
Rostock

Minus twenty-two degrees Fahrenheit drove the country folks into cities and bound the sea under steel-hard ice. The cattle had been herded into warm timber stalls inside the town.

With Rostock harbor in view, Rebane lay flattened on her stomach atop the dune and surveyed her target through the binoculars. The wind ruffled the frozen grass and the air smelled of firewood. Smoke coiled from the chimneys of the town—its houses spread out in an irregular pattern around the airbase.

The greenhouses hibernated under layers of insulation—green salad, peas, potatoes...

Anything grows here.

Rebane watched a woman visit the henhouse at the back of her yard and return with a basketful of eggs.

Yes, scrambled eggs, please.

The survivors in the nuked zones were lucky if a tuft of grass turned green during the summer.

You've got more food than you can eat.

Twenty-five years had passed since an American Cobalt-60 salted hydrogen bomb had detonated above Stockholm. The deliberate hit on the Oskarshamn nuclear plant had rendered the Buffer Zone uninhabitable for centuries. Productive land had been reduced into one percent of what it had used to be.

Fuck! That's not fair.

She tilted her head back and finished her vodka in four long pulls. The deserted villages in Poland and Germany offered plenty of loot. Rebane experienced no guilt breaking into farmhouses and taking what she needed—clothes, batteries, shelter, maps...and alcohol.

Warmth spread into her chest as the vodka diluted her alarm. Rebane hadn't sobered up since she'd dodged the helicopter. She ran northwest through the nights and hid from drones all day until dusk killed the light. But the most challenging task lay ahead and she had only four bullets left. Without the dead soldier's gear, Weisser's men would have caught her long ago. The arctic outfit was a perfect blend with the badlands. When she covered her head with the hood and stayed still, she fooled even the foxes who had the keenest senses.

Just do your last duty and vanish.

Skis would triple her speed, and speed was the defining factor between surviving and perishing. If the winter progressed, she would freeze to death trying to find a safe place. Entering the city was her only hope.

I can't wait to get rid of the file, the last string still connecting me to Weisser's plan.

Rebane studied the wasp's nest through the binoculars. The night vision was of poor quality by Russian standards. The IR didn't work at all. The airstrip, the helipad and the warehouses reminded her of the life she'd left behind. Camo tarps flapped in the wind. Coils of barbed wire crowned the net fence and guard posts housed machine gun stations. Darkness rolled over the land and the airfield lit brighter than the city, its searchlights combing the sky. Rebane wore a worried expression and felt the rush of fear.

A mouse couldn't get in undetected.

The wind carried the sound of a helicopter approaching and she tensed. Rebane recognized the Sikorsky Black Hawk that could take an electromagnetic hit and still keep flying. Powerful rotors whipped the snow, flattened the grass as the dragonfly hovered over the helipad and touched down. The pilot killed the motor and the airfield swarmed with soldiers in camo and mechanics in fur-trimmed winter overalls. Cargo erupted onto the helipad and trucks arrived to move it. Thunder filled the air and a Boeing C-17 Globemaster III landed further away on the full-length airfield. The monster gave birth to countless ammo crates and lock-bolted containers. The multitude of equipment made Rebane's skin crawl.

I'll be on foot and they'll hunt me with Skidoos.

No way in hell would she storm down there alone armed with a 9mm pistol and four bullets. But then her thoughts returned to Frau Engel, a widow who worked as a housekeeper for the commanding officer of the base.

Rebane scanned beyond the airfield perimeter. A brick house stood at the end of a road, surrounded by trees of the garden now undressed from leaves. The more she processed her mad plan, the faster her heart leaped into her throat.

Maybe Weisser's men already surveilled the letterbox. What if it's a trap? Perhaps the whole network worked for him.

Rebane decided to take another look at the airfield communication to see if the Union had satellites to direct a nuclear missile. She zoomed in on the antennae but couldn't pinpoint a telltale satellite dish atop the roofs. Nothing pointed to the atmosphere.

Plain old analog. Weisser lied to me.

Most of the satellites had died because of the EMP or lack of maintenance after the nuclear war. She pursed her lips.

I should just dig a hole for the file and leave.

She put her hand into the bag and felt for the file with her fingers but she couldn't bring herself to take it out.

No. I'm still a soldier and I have my duties.

Sneaking nearer to the outermost peasant houses by the beach, she crossed the silent fields. The snow and the wind combined their forces to harden the fabrics of her clothes. Rebane climbed over the fence and hid behind the animal shed, where she picked the smell of pig dung. Growing restless, the animals shuffled their straw bedding. Rebane reeked of blood which made the pigs oink in alarm.

I smell like a pile of dead rats. I must wash before I meet Engel.

She opened the door with a screech. Inside, a storm lantern offered meager light. The pigs lifted their heads. Putting her finger on her bottom lip, she whispered, "Shhh!"

Their folded ears moved as their snouts picked up her smell but the oinking ceased. She returned outside to check if anything was worth taking.

From the shadows, she watched how the German family gathered around the kitchen table for supper. The house had only one room and the building needed repair, but Rebane smelled the cooked millet and beetroot as she crept nearer. The light which escaped from the window painted the snow yellow. The scene inside stung her heart. The mother ruffled her son's hair as the boy grabbed a large slice of bread, its crust sprinkled with sesame seeds. The snow creaked under Rebane's shoes as she moved closer, keeping well outside the sphere of light.

From the clothesline, she stole a black scarf, a baize skirt, and a wool sweater. She found a basket of frostbitten potatoes—her excuse in case someone demanded a reason for her to sneak into the commander's house.

She crouched to enter the pigsty. In the nearest pen, a pile of piglets cuddled on clean straw. An enormous sow stared back at Rebane. She moved slowly, not wanting to scare the four-hundred-pound mother.

I know you're smart. Don't be afraid. I'll just borrow some of your water.

The sow sniffed her arm with a moist touch of her snout as she closed her fingers around the handle of the water bucket. She used her free arm to offer a potato. The pig smacked as she ate, and Rebane lifted the bucket.

While the animals stared, Rebane got undressed and folded her uniform over the pigsty wall. The water jammed her breath.

"Goddammit, it's cold!"

She scrubbed every inch of her skin, shivering, her teeth clattering.

With the local woman's clothes on, she felt warm. The camouflage jacket and pants went into the bottom of the basket. Rebane placed the pistol in the canvas bag for a fast grab and knotted the thick scarf under her chin. If she remembered to keep her head down the shawl would cover her oriental features. The pigs consumed most of the potatoes, and the rest she arranged as a top layer to hide her gear in the basket. As she petted the sow's head, she allowed her to lift one of the piglets into her lap for a cuddle.

"You're a cute little thing, aren't you," she lisped and kissed the piglet.

I'm going to buy a pig when I get home. And chickens.

Rebane returned the piglet to its mother with a sigh.

Assuming the shape of a peasant woman, she closed the squeaky gate and trotted along the sidewalk.

More rundown houses lined the road, some in ruins. The roof of one cottage had collapsed, but the lights were on, proving someone still lived there. Rebane stayed away from the illuminated windows and dove into the shadows.

She heard the drunken soldiers before they came into view, hovering in the middle of the road. Cold air got caught in her throat.

It's too late to run.

She hopped over the cobblestones, trying to escape to the other side of the street. They stopped singing a dirty song and crossed over to her side. Hairs rose on her neck. Her blood pumped faster as Rebane's hand searched for the pistol's butt. She lined her index finger on the Glock's trigger guard. The first bullet rested inside the chamber. She recognized their uniforms—the European Union navy.

Don't make me shoot. I don't want to cause a scene.

She rushed forward and swooped between their massive bodies, her shoulders hitting against them, each a head and shoulders taller than her.

"Pretty girl, why out so late?" one soldier drawled. "Looking for fun?"

Maybe the gang meant no harm, but Rebane ran. The baize skirt hugged her feet and almost tripped her.

Their voices distanced. "Come on, Fräulein, we have money. We'll pay a fair price," one of them yelled.

She didn't stop running until she reached the edge of the city. Rebane paused by the beach to catch her breath. A gust of wind smelled of fish and ozone, dropping snow from the naked trees as if something walked invisible among them. The sea was a wall of darkness. She clutched her hands together when she found the road toward the manor.

Maybe I should turn back.

The wind resisted her progress as she struggled uphill. Knotting the scarf tighter, Rebane felt a sinking in her stomach. The susurrus of the wind moved through the winter garden as she walked among the hibernating flower beds. The wind brushed her trail as the waves wiped footprints from the sand. She surveilled the commander's house, hiding under the frigid apple trees in the far corner of the garden. Silhouettes moved in the light behind the curtains. Rebane kept an eye on the kitchen window and the servants' entrance.

What if Weisser had gotten to her?

Rebane paced around, too excited to sit down on the stone bench. She fished an ink pen and memo pad from the basket, items snatched from the pigsty windowsill where the matron kept a record of her pedigreed animals. Rebane wrote her coded message on a blank page with neat lettering:

Dear Madame,

I am sorry I couldn't approach you sooner. I've been ill with a bad case of winter flu. Also, there is trouble at the factory. The weaving machine B11 is broken, and we wait for spare parts. I am sorry your skirt fabric wasn't ready for your granddaughter's wedding. Please name the discount price with which you would be happy and give it to the messenger boy. I hope you will continue to speak highly of our services in the future.

With friendly Greetings,
Herr S. Müller

The lines spelled the havoc which the enemy had caused throughout the resistance network and the Russian task force. Frau Engel would understand the last agent's plea for help. Rebane blanched and her hands trembled.

I should go now.

But she forced herself to write *Frau Engel* and the address on the folded paper and slip it into the manor letterbox. Rebane retreated into the shadows and waited in untouched silence until midnight—the hour of contact. A branch with frozen apples curved above her head and the sky cleared, only to cower behind a wall of blizzard moments later.

Hellbent weather for me to ski on the open ice. But the enemy won't get airborne during the storm.

Rebane tensed when a lean shadow of a woman emerged from the servants' door like clockwork. She watched her follow the narrow path across the garden. The elderly woman stood under the front porch's light now, stomping snow from her soles. Frau Engel looked over her shoulder before she opened the lid of the letterbox with a trembling hand. She unfolded the paper and her shoulders bunched. As she read the coded message, Rebane waited with bated breath, the clouds of mist ceasing to appear above her head.

Rebane observed her high cheekbones and the symmetrical features of her narrow face as Engel turned to gaze into the darkness to see if the messenger was still around. Frau Engel was still a beautiful woman at the age of eighty, her white hair knotted into a tight bun. She must have been a dazzler in her youth. Her outline became edgy and she didn't write a reply message. She exhibited fear in her jerky movements as she retreated up the concrete stairs, stuffing the letter into her skirt pocket.

"No, no! Please don't go," Rebane shouted and stepped forward.

"Who is it?" Engel inquired, squinting her eyes.

Rebane moved closer until she stood near enough to touch the woman and they showered in the light. Engel retreated until her back was against the iron railing at the top of the stairs. Rebane removed the scarf and the women faced each other.

"Number 1429," Engel said with a quiver in her voice. «It can›t be. You're dead. Your whole team is dead."

A curl escaped the Frau's bun and she tucked it behind her ear with a delicate move, an instinct. Then the spell broke and the woman dashed for the door, but Rebane was faster. She encased Engel's thin wrist in an iron hold.

"Please, they're watching the house," Engel said in a shrill tone. Her eyes stared wild into the darkness as she tried to squirm free. Rebane could tell the old woman was terrified but forced the nuclear blueprint into her free hand.

"Just pass it along. That's all," Rebane whispered and let go.

Engel had the aura of a broken spirit. Rebane could see the scar which ran across her throat. The paper-like skin of her hand bore the telltale twin burn marks of an electric cattle prod. Engel tucked the file under her arm but would probably toss it to the fireplace first thing when she got inside.

"Look, I don't have much time," Rebane said and hated how her voice revealed her irritation. "I need your help to get a Geiger meter and army-grade skis from the base. I must also get my hands on a sniper rifle." Her heart pounded in her throat.

You must help me.

Frau Engel's hand rested on the door handle, and she turned her back on Rebane. The old woman stood there, her shoulders shaking. She said, "I can't help you. God, I can't even help myself. The whole network has been wiped out. You're on your own."

"Can't you help me sneak onto the base?" Rebane demanded.

Before Engel could say no, someone dropped a kettle in the kitchen and the Frau jumped in fear. Rebane melted into the shade of the apple tree.

"I'm sorry," Engel whispered into the dark. "I was a brave woman once."

There was a time when Rebane would have stabbed anyone who betrayed their cause, but now she simply replied, "I believe you. Just get that file to the Russians."

"Don't worry," Engel added. "I won't tell anyone that I saw you alive."

Frau Engel remained frozen on the top step like a garden statue when Rebane turned around and left.

"Wait," the woman exclaimed. "I think you should know that the Russians have offered ten thousand euros for your head. That's a lot for a ghost, don't you think?"

But the sea breeze had already swallowed Rebane. Engel closed the door behind her.

14.
Airbase

The unmarked navy airplane flew above Germany where the villages slumbered under blackout. When the belly hatch forced open, Rebane's team faced the unknown, twelve-thousand-feet below. Air swirled around the aircraft, making the hull vibrate. Rebane hung onto the cord loop while she waited for the jump signal. She prayed there was no air defense artillery. Adjusting her rucksack straps, she looked over her shoulder at Daniil, the next in line to HALO-parachute behind enemy lines. The Spetsnaz, members of the GRU Special Operations Forces, would open their parachutes at a low altitude after freefalling. Daniil looked like an insect in his helmet, goggles, and oxygen mask—a handsome insect with muscles rippling under the fabric of his night-black tactical outfit.

Concentrate, Second Lieutenant Nordstrom!

"Five minutes to drop!" The pilot's voice buzzed into her headset.

We were a bunch of idiots.

Rebane sighed with frustration. Two hours of surveillance and she still didn't know how to get inside the Rostock airbase undetected. She sought perfection in her plans and obsessed with every detail. Frau Engel could have informed on her despite her promise to keep her mouth shut.

Every minute Rebane spent here endangered her life. The only useful piece of intel was the location of the weapons warehouse at the back of the base's premises where enemy personnel struggled against the whiplashes of polar air to unload the ammo crates. At the same time, the tempest rebuilt dunes onto the airstrip, and the plow trucks were losing the battle.

Think! I didn't survive the nuclear war to die in Rostock.

Rebane took a bite of the military-grade energy bar and lifted the binoculars. She watched a fresh shift of military policemen signaled a truck to stop at the base gates. The pair of them, now glowing green with her night vision switched on, climbed onto the pallet. A traffic jam developed down the road because working in this kind of record blizzard was slow.

Too much action for a standard night shift.

"You're preparing an offensive," Rebane muttered to herself. The sky clouded into a mass of darkness. The wind picked up and promised foul weather.

No wonder they're in a hurry to get the supplies inside.

Her fingertips had lost feeling, and she knew from experience that the defrosting process involved pain. She formed a fist inside the glove, pressing her fingers against the inside of her palm for warmth. She blew onto her fingertips, relieving the ache of returning blood flow before she took another look at the entry point.

A group of women on foot crisscrossed among the cars. The road was well-lit against the wall of white now descending from the sky. Looking straight into the searchlight blinded Rebane through the NVG. She rubbed her eyelids while flashes danced across the field of her vision. When she looked again, one of the truck drivers had rolled down his side window, leaning out. A petite woman resisted the flurry. Removing her scarf, she let the storm ruffle a cloud of blonde curls. Bargaining ensued, and both parties accompanied the negotiations with the movement of their hands. The blonde lifted her skirt to flash a bare leg. The wind had a ferocious bite and Rebane couldn't understand how the whore didn't shiver.

The boom lifted. One of the policemen whistled when the truck didn't move. The girl walked with a swinging gait, moving her hips from side-to-side, and a swarm of catcalls escorted her across the yard.

That's my way in.

More women arrived and the hustle began in earnest. The body language of the guards relaxed. They even let the next vehicles enter without searching the cargo.

I don't need much of an act to fool those horny bastards.

The guards grew weary in the cold, chain-smoking and loitering against the boom. The pistol went under the waistband of the matron's skirt. She left the basket and her winter war outfit at the hideout. Rebane pinched her cheeks and bit her lips for a healthy red as she descended the hillside. She hopped onto the tarmac behind the curve in the road. The winter scarf blocked the current of air coming from the harbor and Rebane kept her head low. Her palms sweated inside her mittens. The guards had their backs toward her.

You can still turn and run.

The stockier one glanced over his shoulder and elbowed his comrade. She kept her eyes on the younger man, like a lioness on the hunt makes a tactical assessment to select her target. Her steps tapped on the icy tarmac. Rebane forced herself to breath shallowly, convinced they would notice her agitation.

"How much?" The older man with the potbelly asked when she stood in front of the boom. As broad as he was tall, he towered above her.

"Sixty euros for special treatment," she whispered, still staring at her shoes. Rebane felt the bulge of the Glock under her elbow.

"It's too much. He won't pay that much," the younger man commented while he patted himself in the bitterly cold breeze. Wood crackled in the subzero air and their breaths misted above their heads. Rebane resisted a shiver.

"Hmmm. Who then, Liebchen?" Rebane asked and looked at the youngster.

He had acne on his cheeks and the tall, skinny frame of an adolescent who'd had to grow up too fast.

"The Commandant," the older man cut in, blinking with colorless eyelashes. "He's throwing a party for the officers tonight. You're late, Fräulein." He stroked Rebane's cheek, and she jolted with repulsion. His hand stopped midmotion as the watchtower bathed the trio in the searchlight.

"You're not German," he said, suspicion in his voice. His deep-brown cow's eyes never left Rebane's face and she could tell he was wondering about the bruises.

"War loot from the conquered zones, Mein Herr," Rebane purred. She found the right gear and added, "Maybe your handsome friend fancies an eastern flavor?" The moon of the guard's face melted into a smile, and Rebane assured herself that the potbelly had bought the story.

She opened her scarf. Running her hand through her sheer black mane, Rebane pressed against the youngster. When he didn't know how to react, she directed his hand under her sweater. The young man shivered more than she did when his cold fingers closed around her naked breast.

"Have you fucked anyone like me before?" Rebane asked, licking her lips.

"Uli hasn't fucked anyone before," potbelly said, chuckling. "He came straight from the virgin factory." The older man laughed at his own joke.

Red as a beetroot, Uli glared at potbelly, who gave him the thumbs up.

"I'll pay for it," the older man said and rubbed his neck where excess fat formed a fold above his uniform collar. "It's time you had some fun, Mein Freund. Fuck the officers. They have more girls than they can handle." He took out his wallet and nailed Rebane with his gaze. "I know this is just the right girl to make you a man. I remember a campaign back east...let's just say we took what we wanted."

Rebane thought of leading potbelly into the slaughterhouse instead but trying to manhandle the more experienced guard was a risk.

No, he could overpower me.

She touched potbelly's arm and said, "You can pay me afterward, when your friend is happy." She nodded toward Uli.

Hunger flickered in potbelly's eyes. "There's a first time for everything, Mein Freund," he said. "For a dirty whore who doesn't demand that we pay beforehand and for you to get laid."

Rebane wanted to take out her double-edged blade and teach potbelly manners. But she controlled the urge.

"Maybe I can have a go, too?" The older man suggested as his hand traced Rebane's throat into the dimple between her collar bone. Completely bald, he also lacked eyebrows to arch. "What do you think, Uli?"

Rebane forced herself to endure the touch of his greasy fingers. She suppressed a memory that immediately surfaced and shifted her gaze to Uli.

Uli broke the ice by placing his long arm around Rebane's shoulders. He squeezed her against his body and Rebane feared he would feel the butt of her pistol or the handle of the blade. Uli pushed his cap back. Ruffling his ginger buzz cut, the young man smiled.

Must be the top of his date moves, Rebane guessed.

"I'll take care of you, lover, but one stud at a time, right?" She managed to wink at potbelly as she took Uli's hand and led him toward the warehouses, but he came to a sudden halt. Misty puffs rose above his head and he breathed a shade faster. Rebane shivered, freezing without the layer of padded camo under her disguise.

"What?" she asked.

"Wait. I can't leave my post."

He broke free and marched back to the guard shack. The two men stood talking under the light. Rebane retreated into the shadow of the warehouse, praying this one had the rifle she needed. Her thighs and buttocks tingled in the cutting breeze. The baize skirt and the wool stockings couldn't keep the cold at bay.

Come back, come back now…

Uli pointed at her, and the potbelly took out his walkie talkie. She couldn't hear what he said. Fear clutched her entrails.

It's my face. My damned face…

"Can't you get someone else to cover for you?" she shouted at Uli, but he didn't respond.

A door of the administrative building opened, cutting into the darkness. A third man walked across the yard, taking his time finishing a cigarette. He waved his hand and Uli launched forward, running toward Rebane. The snow creaked under his boots as he arrived, out of breath and beaming with anticipation. Uli stepped over the snowbank and glued himself onto her without warning. He kissed her with clumsy force, ramming her against the warehouse wall. She reminded herself not to twist his nuts.

Slow down.

Uli's tongue slipped between her lips and sloppy, deep kisses ensued as he guided her hand onto the hardening bulge between his legs.

The guards can see us.

"It's too cold outside, Liebchen," Rebane said as she came up for air.

And Uli stopped…just like that. He reached for the key chain around his neck and opened the warehouse door. The lights switched on automatically. Rebane shunned the surveillance camera by instinct but Uli didn't connect the dots.

"Don't worry. The camera doesn't work," he said, but Rebane froze, nonetheless.

He lifted her on top of a crate and pinned her down with his weight. Rebane felt the heat of his body. Her thighs tensed when Uli positioned himself between her legs and lifted her skirt. His breath raced as he found her panties and ripped them down. She felt like a stone plunging into a well.

No!

She struggled to keep her voice steady. "Wait. Wait. Let me show you what I can do with my mouth first. It's my specialty, lover."

He understood and lifted his weight. His youthful face flushed a deep red. Uli looked as if he would explode any minute.

"Okay. Do your worst," Uli whispered. His eyes clouded with lust.

He opened his belt buckle with a chink against the crate and unzipped his trousers. The wind from the sea howled among the roof trusses and rocked the lamps thirty feet above their heads. Rebane kneeled in front of his erection and Uli closed his eyes, anticipating her mouth.

What a pity.

Rebane lifted her sweater, her hands forming a point forward hold around the knife's handle. When Uli arched his neck, she plunged the knife into his groin. The double-edged blade entered halfway in, severing the large arteries. Rebane turned her face away to avert the spill of blood, but the warmth from Uli's body squirted onto her throat.

He didn't utter a sound. Uli didn't understand something was wrong before he felt the wetness between his thighs. The tip of the blade had hit his femoral bone. Rebane moved to the side, twisting the knife out. Ruby-red arterial blood showered from the wound as his heart picked up pace and tried to compensate for his plummeting blood pressure.

Rebane watched in a dreamlike state as he staggered backward. Detached, she observed how the youngster slumped onto the floor and placed his hands over the outpouring. His heart squirted more blood between his fingers. Uli quickly lost consciousness and his muscle tone slackened. He stopped breathing, but his baby-blue eyes remained open, fixated onto Rebane. She was the last thing Uli ever saw.

Like an automaton, she wiped the blade onto his winter coat before sheathing it. The crawlers and Skidoos lined the walls, parked in neat rows, and painted with arctic camo patterns. Their inclined headlamps stared at her like predatory eyes. Rebane yanked out of her trance with a jolt of terror.

You used too much time. Move!

Rebane retrieved Uli's keys. None fit into the locks on the crates. She ran along the corridor, peeking onto pallet racks loaded with spare parts, power batteries and tools. The wire partitions housed items packed in black plastic, but they were too bulky to house weapons. It was a mechanic's workshop.

The wrong warehouse!

She grabbed a torchlight and battled to open the door against the wind and the snow. Outside, her breath misted in the cold night. She used snow to wash some of Uli's blood from her hands. Her sweater was soaked with the viscous substance and the smell of the slaughterhouse attacked her senses. The wind rattled the tin roof. The blizzard snuffed the lights of Rostock and the guards stayed indoors. Even the glowworm of trucks into the base had ceased. Uli's keyring slipped from her grasp and sank into powdered snow.

Clumsy idiot!

Rebane shook with suppressed rage, lifted her bloodied sleeve, and hooked the frozen keys.

Her earlobes numbed in the wind, and she decided to raid the next warehouse while her incredible luck lasted. Finding the right key, she slipped inside. Rebane lit the torchlight when the light in the ceiling didn't obey the switch. She bit her bottom lip. Her breath got caught in her throat as the surveillance camera auto-zoomed on her. The device rotated at the end of a robotic lever, following Rebane's every move.

Fuck! Too late to hide my face.

All armies shared the same manner of organizing their equipment, and it didn't take her long to locate the rifles. Rebane found a 50mm monster but it didn't suit the purpose of traveling light. She ran along the corridor scanning cabinets and shelves while her head rushed with adrenaline. The veins in Rebane's neck ticked.

Too slow!

She ran her fingers across the stocks of semiautomatic assault rifles and machine guns, all of them secured with locks and chains.

A gunsmith's station...it must be here.

Against the back wall, she found a gunsmith's turning machinery, his collimator, and the ammunition press. The scent of gun oil greeted her. The cabinet doors remained unlocked, and several rifles lay on the table polished and assembled for the range. Her heart lifted when Rebane spotted the jackpot—a Finnish Tikka T3X TAC A1 with a lightweight body. The sniper's scope and the silencer all painted matte-black and worth more than Dad's farm and Rebane's life combined.

With eager hands, she handled the Tikka. She removed the lock bolt to check the bore. The grooves spiraled flawlessly. Inserting the bolt, Rebane pushed the lever without any resistance. A disarming smile spread onto her lips.

Engineered precision, the best I could find!

Pressing the trigger caused the rifle to expel an obedient click and assured her the old weapon worked as if they'd manufactured it yesterday. All her movements were swift and professional. This was her element. Rebane filled her pockets and the canvas bag with Win. 308 bullets—as many as she could carry. She loaded the clip with nimble hands. The first cartridge entered the chamber, and she pressed the safety button on. Rebane fixed a synthetic strap onto the corresponding rings and slung the heavy firearm onto her back.

She listened behind the door before stepping outside amidst the whirlwind of snow. Satisfied, she turned to lock the door.

A slight pressure pressed at the nape of her neck—the unmistakable touch of a barrel. Her heart thudded, pounding in her ears.

The path crunched like sugar underfoot as the man said, "Raise your hands above your head and turn around slowly."

15.
Sea Ice—Part I

"Raise your hands above your head and turn around slowly," he said.

Rebane obeyed and faced potbelly. The muzzle of his assault rifle hovered at the level of her eyes.

"Where's Uli?" he demanded.

Rebane maintained eye contact but didn't reply. The barrel dropped a notch and potbelly stood too near for his safety. He saw the Tikka Rebane had strapped onto her back.

"What are you doing with the rifle, whore?" he barked.

She took a step forward and her arms lowered.

"Stop right there," potbelly commanded as the muzzle touched Rebane's forehead. Her eyes narrowed into slits as she searched for something to divert the guard's attention.

A thought occurred to her.

If you'd wanted to kill me, you would have already shot me.

She shifted her weight and opened her stance for balance.

Wham! A gust of wind whacked the warehouse door against the wall and Rebane ducked while lifting the barrel above her head. The gun went off because potbelly had his finger on the trigger. She ignored the pain the explosion caused in her ears and thrust the base of her palm into his larynx. The guard staggered back. His eyes bulged as he struggled to breathe and his fleshy face reddened.

Rebane pointed his own rifle at him. "You'll survive the punch," she lied. "You'll be able to breathe within a few minutes. Tell me where the skis are, or I'll shoot you." Her head swam with adrenaline.

Potbelly held his throat with plump hands, his lips trying to formulate a word. Only a rasp emerged from his collapsed windpipe as he imitated a fish on dry land.

She cleared her throat. "Point! This is your last chance," Rebane yelled over the wild wind.

He indicated the next warehouse. With hope in her eyes, Rebane waded through three feet of snow, frostbite nibbling at her toes. The sky washed with grey and the ground wore the color of the blank page.

Rebane spotted a pair of fiberglass skis leaning against the wall by the door.

She picked up one for a closer inspection. The nose was broad and would slow her speed but would offer a better lift in deep snow. The base had no lubrication wax, and the polyethylene was littered with scratches, but the skis housed old-style binds she could attach to any shoe. Rebane discarded the newer cross-country set which demanded ski boots for a fit. The poles were a mismatch as well—one an inch shorter than its pair. Rebane battled to open the buckles of the multipurpose boot-binding.

"For fuck's sake!" Her shoe size was too small, and she had to improvise.

An electric sizzle preceded the scent of burning wire. The airstrip went dark and a power failure snuffed the streetlights along the beach road one by one.

Forget the Geiger meter. Your time is up.

She wrapped the grip straps around her gloves. The basket of the pole seemed suitable for the terrain ahead and the carbide tip sharp enough. The skis moved with smooth speed on the level ground but offered no grab while ascending. With a free skate style, she reached the body of potbelly. His darkened tongue hung out of his mouth.

Dead as a rock.

Rebane tried to see if the guards were around the shack. Her hair raised and her blood pumped faster. There was no way to make sure in the dark and she had left her NV binoculars at the hideout.

Stupid!

Getting out required a leap of faith—sliding down the slope blind.

With a diagonal skate, Rebane reached the top of the ridge above the airfield. She crouched and spread her legs to gather momentum and rushed downhill. She almost hit Uli's wingman, who stepped out of the guard shack as she swooshed by. Rebane bent double with an estimate to fit under the boom and aimed for the middle of the road.

"Hey!" the man screamed after her.

With the wind in her ears, she expected to hear the ra-ta-ta of his assault rifle, but he never opened fire. The arctic night embraced her and the terrorist who'd killed two men vanished.

Rebane formed the V-shape, the tips of her skis touching for a halt where the plowed tarmac started. She opened the binds and carried both skis on her shoulder. With weak legs, she reached her lookout spot and undressed like a snake shedding its skin. The full winter gear wrapped her with warmth and she crammed the bloody peasant disguise into the canvas bag.

It may come handy again.

Putting on her skis, she rattled off, the slope helping her reach the bay where the force of the storm attacked her head on. At the end of the horseshoe curve, she turned to face the city of Rostock once more.

"Rot in peace, Europe," Rebane screamed as her side stung from the strain. "I hope we never meet again!" The night engulfed her primal scream and the streetlights lining the beach road blinked on and off for a final goodbye. A vigorous headwind robbed her speed on the ice. Two hundred miles of flatness with no cover lay ahead.

Ilmatar, goddess of the Air, let the storm last. Hide my trail from the pursuers.

Rebane knew she couldn't see ice crevasses before hurling hundreds of feet into a deathtrap. But she had to gain a head start in the darkness before the Skidoos would hunt her. She realigned her heading to avoid the worst bite of the storm.

Wind like this will brush my trail into oblivion before the dawn.

Using her triceps, Rebane pushed with the poles and kept her legs aligned for a classic technique. The fiberglass skis sliced a track into the wind-beaten snow and with the storm behind her back now, she added to her pace. The ice binding the waves of the Baltic Sea wasn't smooth. The grooves crisscrossed like veins on top of a man's arm. Sweat broke from her back and the wind pulled Rebane's hood down. She stopped anew to tie its cord in a double knot. Pulling her coat sleeves over her mittens, Rebane crossed a rough patch using the V-style. The skis didn't offer enough grip to continue with the classic approach.

I'd give anything for some temperature-rated kick wax.

She curled her toes inside the shoes, but nothing could stop the numbing. The skin over her nose felt tight and thin. Rebane adjusted her gloves to leave a pocket of warm air around her fingertips. Already, her toes pricked with a particular pain. She had to do something about the shoes, which offered no insulation.

A flurry of snow swirled around her. Rebane took out her knife and cut strips of fabric from the hem of the pig woman's skirt. She removed her shoes and wrapped the baize around her socks. Her toes had become like pieces of rock. She did jumping-jacks to get her blood flowing before she reattached the ski binds.

The breeze created ripples in the snow. The storm raised snowdrifts as high as mountains and leveled them the next moment. Made of air, the Spirit of Ilmatar walked barefoot on the frozen masses of saltwater. The wind was the ancestral origin of the Nenets people, but what hid Rebane from the eye in the sky could also kill her. The combination of wind speed and temperature, now creating minus forty-nine degrees Fahrenheit, could sever the blood flow into Rebane's extremities and cause sepsis.

I must keep moving.

Rebane's strength drained after midnight. The gusts ripped the ragged clouds apart and a waxing gibbous moon revealed its face. The scenery could be the face of the moon and Rebane hadn't yet found a hideout. The light faded into a gray fog with puffs of wind from the north. The temperature plummeted. An area of high air pressure would bring excellent visibility—and death.

Her heartbeat slowed into a lazy drumroll against her ribs and she resisted the urge to lie down for an hour or two. Sleepiness was a symptom of hypothermia. Rebane had stopped for a pee three times during the last hour. A clump of ice beneath the powder caused her to stumble. She didn't even flinch from the pain in her knee. Her brain urged her to rest or she would die from fatigue, but she knew better.

If I go to sleep her, I'll never wake again.

16.
Sea Ice—Part II

A pockmarked moon remained in the Western sky despite the first light. The sun appeared low, with blazing orange that bled into the crevasses. A pink-blue hue, which Rebane knew as a sign of a cold, lucid day, predicted doom. When she leaned on the carbon-fiber poles to catch her breath, she couldn't help but admire the snowdrifts, now painted with vigorous brushstrokes.

If I die here, so be it. At least the place is gorgeous.

She listened. Because the wind had died, visibility was clear for miles. Nothing appeared out of place but her brows scrunched together.

They will come, make no mistake about that.

She fished the last dehydrated military meal from her baggage and studied the plastic material.

Impressive stuff. They should start producing this again.

But no one wasted oil to make plastic anymore. Whomever had prepared Pavel, the smuggler for the voyage, knew what he was doing. If she survived long enough to trade in the Container City, that translucent wrap would sell within five seconds.

Rebane hadn't slept during the night, but as she checked the compass and the map, she knew it was the right call. She should see the tree line of Gedser, Denmark soon. The skis had quadrupled her speed.

I'll bet I can secure ski boots and better skis if I make it to Sweden.

Rapidly ascending, the sun turned the scenery into polished silver and made Rebane pray for sun goggles—or clouds. Traveling through the blaze could cause snow blindness and render her helpless. A splash interrupted her thoughts and air caught in her throat. The pistol appeared in her hand before she'd even acknowledged her actions. Shading her eyes, she saw a seal pup slack by a breathing hole, fat and clumsy. Rebane pondered shooting and skinning the silver-furred baby but drying a pelt with salt and scrubbing took ages. Too late, the animal went for a nosedive. Another splash and it was beyond the hunter's reach.

As a soldier of the arctic, Rebane knew that cold weather suppressed thirst and dehydration increased the danger of hypothermia. Rebane couldn't risk making a fire and melted snow in her mouth instead.

Weisser must have watched the security tape at some point.

Pushing her hood down, Rebane straightened her back. The wind had died, leaving the track of her skis easily traceable. Turning her head, she picked up the sound of an insistent whirring.

A drone?

She saw nothing but chunks of packed ice, menthol blue and the chrome of the snowfield. The noise stopped, leaving only the tempo of her pulse in her ears. A black dot danced above the horizon, only to disappear as Rebane blinked the water from her eyes and refocused. The buzz returned and the dot grew into a spider with double rotors and skids.

Yup, a drone.

The machine changed direction, sped up to approach from her flank. It was too late now to evade her pursuers with traditional techniques. She turned the zoom turret of her rifle's scope and pushed the bolt lock forward. With her thumb on the safety button of the Tikka, she took aim. The drone braked to hover above and the burring took on a higher note. The twin cameras stared at her—remote-controlled and unerring.

They found me.

The 1X view was more than enough. She focused her crosshairs. The operator attempted a swift retreat to save the drone, but the most candid shot of Rebane's career punctured the machine's body. The motor stalled and the drone plopped into white powder next to Rebane's shoe, its rotors slurring into a swan song. She unbuckled the binds of her skis so she could stomp the machine to death, grinding her teeth. "Fucking clear weather!"

With a turn of the turret for a 6X zoom and a rush of adrenaline, Rebane scanned the northern skyline. Her heart missed a beat as she returned her sights upon a formation of jagged shapes. The fir trees of Denmark were transfixed darker against the interplay of sky and ice. She estimated the distance was five to six miles. A lazy gust of wind herded a slither of snow and the sky remained naked without a hint of clouds.

If they have a helicopter I won't get to the forest.

The ice between her and the shore splintered and going around the cracks would take double time. Rebane decided her only hope was a heap of snow nine hundred feet to the right. A group of boulders formed from frozen saltwater leaned on each other's shoulders. Behind them roamed a stretch of the open sea.

Worth a try.

She V-styled for her life until the snow became too deep. Rebane carried the skis on her shoulder and removed her gear. Five to six feet of packed snow was enough to stop the enemy bullets and the blocks formed an extra obstacle. On all fours, she looked for a place to drill an embrasure. Worry hit her like a bag of stones and sweat trickled down her spine. Rebane ran her fingers between the chunks of ice and measured the height for a lying prone position. As the blade cut through, she worked in a frenzy to make the hole big enough for the silencer.

Time...I don't have enough time.

She paused work to listen, but only drifting powder snow moved around her—no oscillating or slapping from the rotors of a helicopter.

As she lay on her stomach, the view through the rifle scope exposed nothing but ice. She decided on the 6X magnifying setting to relocate a moving target. Rebane folded the leg notch bipod along the barrel and supported her weapon against the canvas bag. A few punches flattened the top and allowed the Tikka to rest. A bolt lock action rifle stomached the extreme cold of where she was heading, but trouble reloading and finding the target in her sights were downsides. Rebane ran her finger along the trigger guard and wet her lips. Accuracy would decide whether she lived or died. She rechecked the safety button.

Yup. Even so, on.

The Goddess of the Wind hadn't appeared when Rebane needed her protection most. The twin trail of her skis led directly into her hideout.

One hand grenade and I'm mincemeat.

She bit her bottom lip and bolted up. Rebane ripped the peasant clothes from the bag and battled to get the frozen outfit into form. She rubbed her corded neck as she approached the stretch of open sea where sunlight played on the waves. If she brushed away all footprints except the ones leading here...

The perfect ambush.

She sacrificed the blood flow of her bare fingers to dip a handful of snow into the water. The substance became easy to mold when wet, and Rebane filled the baize skirt and the sweater with the stuff. The cold cemented the shape of a woman sitting with her back toward Germany.

Warming her hands inside her pockets allowed Rebane to regain control of her fingers. She formed a snowball and rolled it on powdered snow to add enough mass for the figure's head. After wrapping the scarf over the snowwoman's head, she admired her handiwork. At a distance, the enemy would fall for it.

A perfect decoy. I'll bet they'll waste bullets on my dummy.

Rebane paced back and forth to wipe her tracks. The fluttering in her stomach grew as she assumed her battle position behind the wall. An hour had passed, judging by the sun's steady ascent, before the grey dots started growing in her sights. The enemy came like the wind—three men on snowmobiles but no air support.

Thank you, Spirit of the Red Fox and the Flame.

The roaring of their motors reached her. A current of air blew from Rebane's right flank and she clicked the lateral adjustment turret of her scope to match it. She remained still so as not to disturb the snow and give away her position while the blood in her veins chilled to ice. Each man wore an arctic combat outfit and rode with a rifle strapped to his back. Rebane could see the top layer of their snow camo flapping in the wind, and the bastards wore quality sun goggles. They had switched their headlights off but the sun glinted from the lamps and their skids caused the white powder to catch the wind.

I'll bet they're wearing body armor, but if the protective plates aren't thick enough my .308 will knock a man off his snowmobile.

The enemy was three hundred yards away, riding almost side-by-side. Rebane waited, the excitement curling into a ball inside her chest. The lead driver lifted his arm to signal a slower speed. He gestured toward the dummy and the snowcats scattered, making a rapid succession of shots more difficult. The first driver opened fire, sending a puff of snow skyward beside Rebane's inanimate double.

Rebane drew the rifle stock against her pectoral muscle. All doubt left her as she concentrated on her breathing. The crosshairs centered on the lead driver as her finger depressed the trigger with complete follow-through. The first round met center mass, knocking the man cold turkey from his ride. Rebane opened the bolt on her Tikka rifle and pulled it back far enough to confirm that there was a round in the chamber. The magazine held five rounds of the win .308. She put another bullet through the armpit of the fallen man to make sure he was dead.

The second man released a spray of automatic bursts that chewed through the dummy. Its snowball head rolled off the shoulders and revealed the deception. When the ra-ta-ta of his assault rifle paused, Rebane's bullet took out the second driver through his throat. He slumped against the cockpit as his mouth struggled to gasp for air. He let go of the throttle handle and the snowcat came to a halt.

Before she could get the third snowmobile into her crosshairs, hostile fire hit the boulders and sent splinters of ice flying above her head. Rebane should have crawled to a different location because the Tikka's muzzle flare had given away her sniper's position. She flattened and withdrew the barrel from the embrasure. Rebane's bowels turned to water as she waited for the man's next move. She didn't dare raise her head for a look.

Then there was silence and the growl of an accelerating snowcat. On all fours, Rebane crawled around the wall of ice as her heart bumped against her ribs.

Keep your head down. He will shoot again.

But when the bullets never came, Rebane left the safety of the snow castle. The last Skidoo had made a U-turn instead of fighting back. The driver missed the open water by a few feet and distanced himself at full speed. Rebane assumed a standing position but her eyes watered in the sunlight. The snowcat whipped up snow, offering him the perfect smokescreen.

She ran past victim number one, who lay unmoving, the snow coloring dark red underneath his corpse. With the sunlight behind her, Rebane kneeled for a long-distance shot, but the fleeing man was already six hundred feet away. The silenced Tikka let out a muffled thud after another, but she missed. The wind was strong from the west. Blue smoke coiled from the muzzle, making the hot air vibrate in front of Rebane's sights. What most afflicted her was the knowledge that she'd failed. Biting the inside of her cheek, she decided what to do.

Take what you need and flee for your life.

Rebane collected her nerve and strapped the secured rifle onto her back. She made a stop by victim number two and battled his heavy carcass down from his ride. Grunting from the effort, Rebane removed his snow goggles and hung them around her neck. She mounted his snowcat, and the motor let out a healthy purr when she turned the ignition key. Waves of frustration flooded her mind as Rebane loaded her gear onboard the snowcat.

I never miss my mark!

She'd finished strapping her skis onboard when a sting bothered her lower abdomen. Another wave of pain spasmed inside of her and sweat glued her shirt onto her back. Warmth flooded between Rebane's thighs. Fresh blood stained her fingers when she removed her hand from her trousers. It took her a moment to understand that a bullet fragment hadn't grazed her, but her period had started.

I'm not pregnant!

Rebane's hands pressed into fists as she hissed, "Now gaze upon me, Goddess of the Open Sky, Ilmatar." She lowered her eyes and thought of the depth which roared under the crust of ice. "And Ahti, Master of the Fish and the Abyss, you witness that I, Rebane Nordstrom, shall never give birth to a child." To make her point, she screamed into the wind with all her might.

And now the wind came like a ghost whispering from the west and Rebane rode at full throttle toward Denmark.

17.
Mining Colony

Norway, February 2049

Rebane checked the thermometer. It showed a new record—minus fifty-eight degrees Fahrenheit. She lifted the hood of her reindeer-skin parka before she stepped out of the main building. The entrance of the deserted mine hid between the twin mountains at the far end of the fjord. This had become her refuge for the dead of winter. A bitter wind wailed in the perpetual shadow of the gorge and the windchill stung despite several layers of fur.

Rebane had found a Geiger meter among the ruins of Kristiansand, a ghost city on the southern shore of Norway. Pertti, her stepdad, had taught her a long time ago where to look. She'd entered a medical isotope treatment unit in the city hospital and had even managed to revive the battery with the help of a manual emergency loader. Rebane knew other survivors searched in the same places, but the "zombies," the city dwellers, evaded someone like her. The radiation counter proved that Sweden was still off limits so Rebane, the lone nomad, skied west after the snowcat ran out of fuel. She'd accepted the Norwegian detour.

A pale imitation of daylight persisted from eleven until two outside the mine. No wonder the place was empty and the spy airplanes ceased flight over the No Man's Land. The blue moment spread over the mining colony like a roll of cellophane film at only half-past one in the afternoon. Rebane had just left the mountain's lap when a rumble startled her. The old instinct put the cocked rifle into her hands faster than she could think, but only loose rocks rolled down the mountainside. She wobbled downhill toward the sea. Her snow boots sank into drifts up to her knees as sweat dripped down her back.

Her feeling of safety had changed into loneliness in mid-January. Rebane saw movement from the corner of her eye and shuffling steps traversed across empty rooms the miners had left in disarray. Terrible anxiety followed her, the shadow's clawed fingers just an inch out of reach. She numbed the pain with the whiskey, vodka, wine, cognac, and moonshine she swiped from the workers' shacks. She even drained medical spirits she'd located in the colony hospital.

Three-story brick houses formed the three sides of the square and the ocean controlled the fourth. Nature would soon conquer this manmade refuge. The glacier reached halfway into the square, and ice crawled into the first floor of the seaside houses. The granite eyes of a statue, perhaps the founder of this long-lost enterprise, followed her as she labored on. Out of breath, Rebane decided to sit on the bench, which had grown icicles. The wind attacked from the sea, beating against her clothes, and the air smelled of ozone. As no seals made an appearance, she unscrewed the cap from a bottle of vodka and savored deep gulps with closed eyes. The alcohol worked and her grief yielded like water.

The sky became onyx black within an hour. A rose-gold still lingered on the lower slopes as a last offensive of the dying daylight. Rebane knew this moment by heart—she could feel the veil that separated the dead from the living thin and stretch. The moon's face hid behind the broad shoulder of the Troll Mountain where wind lived as moving snowdrifts. Stars already punctured the darkness above.

No wonder the miners believed in mountain devils. This place makes you see things.

It was dangerous to venture here after dark, but today she couldn't have cared less. Rebane needed to raid the buildings and keep the ghosts at bay. With a burp, she willed herself to rise. Her face raw and eyes squinting from the cold, she noticed the door of the nearest house ajar. The polar bears here were fast and ferocious. Unless she hit the beast's heart with her first shot...

Scary creatures.

She lowered her hood and removed her mittens before climbing inside over the heap of snow. The polar wind tamed into a breeze within the brick walls, but her breath still misted from the cold. The flashlight taped below the Tikka's barrel had plenty of power after she managed to start the diesel aggregate in the main basement. Lighting the way and feeling for the next step, she crossed the hall. Some of the houses could bury her, but pillars like legs of an elephant supported this one. Discarded stuff—clothes and plastic bags, lay everywhere. Trash formed heaps where packs of rats nested. Their eyes gleamed red before the beam of light and caused them to burrow deeper. Sometimes Rebane would hold out a piece of food and the bravest rodent would nib it from her palm.

Her heart leaped into her throat several times. Something restless moved in the dark just beyond the field of her vision. But she couldn't give up now. Rebane fought her way to the kitchen, which was the best place to scavenge. She minded the glass shards and twisted metal. Cardboard insulation hung from the ceiling and the loose bits flapped in the airflow. A swarm of mice ran for cover as she broke the lock of the pantry with the crowbar. Rebane stuffed tin cans into her rucksack—fruit in sugar juice, baked beans, and meat—all excellent choices.

At least I don't have to starve.

The shore was lost in the night as she left the house. Nothing besides the moan of the wind reached her ears. Rebane's lashes froze together in minutes and she buried her hands inside the fur mittens before they could grow numb. The evening arrived cold and dry, perfect for the appearance of *Aurora Borealis,* the Fox Fires. She returned to the icicle bench and sat on her furry bottom. She had manufactured her trousers from three layers of sealskin. The sewing skills Khadne had taught her became handy here on the border zone between the living and the dead.

Rebane opened a jar of moonshine to banish the chill. Switching off the flashlight, she sat mute in the darkness. Everywhere the rising moon could touch, the diamonds of powdered snow sparkled in obedient return. Rebane forced the homemade brew of a dead miner down her throat and blinked the tears out of her eyes. She missed her stepdad's sweet moonshine.

She calmed down when the sky became a dark slate and silence cocooned the bench by the shore. The heat of trouble settled as the red and green bands danced above the mountain range. Rebane tossed the empty bottle away. She didn't feel the ravages of the polar breeze anymore and the heaviness had exited her chest. She grunted as she lowered her set of multiple trousers to urinate in the snow. Too wasted to walk, she reached the last slope before the top of the hill by crawling on all fours. Here, the view spread unobstructed into all directions and the darkness offered the perfect background for nature's light show.

A ledge of crusted snow hung over the highest ridge, gleaming in the silver moonlight. Rebane lay on her back there, not caring if she froze to death or dropped a hundred feet below. The white coating reflected the red of rubies, green of emeralds and the frigid light of diamonds. A billion stars. The arch of the Milky Way above her. Rebane lay on a feather cushion of white powder. The air became alive with light, movement, and color. Blue squirmed and then vanished for an undulating green to take the stage. The bands waved and crisscrossed and a spiked crown formed around the polar north. Lilac flashed forth where blue dissolved into the black. Rebane traced the Aurora Borealis with her mitten and waited.

After midnight, he came forth from nothingness with stars in his fur. The playful *Fire Fox* galloped across the dark velvet. The stories told that whoever hunted this creature would live wealthy and revered for the rest of his life, but Rebane had never willed to kill such absolute beauty.

The heavenly Fox arched his back for a leap, and the hind legs kicked sparkles from the Troll Mountain's slopes. The creature threw his head back while his flames licked the darkness. The fluff of his tail brushed streaks of color, which remained for a while before they vanished. Its white tip whipped the heavens and stroked fire like a lit match wherever it touched.

Rebane cried and the tears froze onto her lashes. Her chest tightened as the split irises focused on her and Fire Fox sat on the mountaintop. The sly smile which all foxes share appeared on the creature's face. The stars still twinkled through the curtain of fire when Rebane raised her hand and the flickering animal allowed her to stroke his head. With the touch of his flame, joy spread into her limbs.

Revontuli—The Fire of the Fox.

She fell asleep and descended through several weightless layers. In her dreams, the Fox covered its nose with his tail as he curled into a ball. Rebane jolted awake once more when the feeling of freefall alarmed her, but she resettled. Her spirit guide glanced at her with amber eyes. Images began passing behind Rebane's eyelids in rapid succession. She transported into the void of sleep and the darkness sang between the mountains.

18.
White Death

A blood-curling roar echoed from the mountain pass. With a sense of help-lessness, Rebane bounced up. Her legs hadn't yet woken up and the feather pillow of snow received her weight as she tumbled into the embankment. Rebane read-ied herself for an attack by removing the clumsy reindeer mittens. She wore fin-gerless wool gloves beneath and felt for the Tikka's trigger guard. Her head rushed with terror as she listened for the enormous paws treading snow. She knew the scope was useless in the twilight before morning. She would have to wait for the animal to appear. Her pupils dilated, but nothing panted heat onto her skin or dripped saliva from a mouth lined with forty-two sharp teeth.

In places, the furrowed rock face lay exposed. Snowflakes drifted into the flurry and the unforgiving wind cut Rebane's face. A handful of snow had entered her collar while she slept and was now melting between the shoulder blades.

Another roar erupted from the direction of the mine. Rebane lifted her hood, which had fallen off, and cursed as she got a shower of the icy stuff. She gazed through the rifle's scope but the northern morning didn't give enough light to spot the location of the white beast. An avalanche traversed into the lap of a mountain somewhere and its rumble slowly died.

Rebane grabbed the army binoculars and switched on the night-vision but her breath clouded the lenses.

Where are you? Show your fat ass, White Death.

She lowered the rifle because the growling sounded nearer now. Neither the naked eye nor the binoculars had revealed its source. The mist cowered at the back of the gorge which dwelled in shadow. Somewhere, pebbles rolled downhill. She checked the beast's favorite spots—trash bins, the landfill, and the beach. Not even a white hair floated around.

Something moved downhill and cast shadows on the snow. An irritated growl, and a polar bear cub stumbled into view. Another leaped onto the first one's back, bit the soft skin of the neck and attempted to thrash its prey.

Helpless babies.

Relief flooded Rebane.

She secured her rifle and shouldered it by the strap. Rebane approached the cubs in a calm pace and a crouching stance. Each time a cub glanced at her she froze. The sniper rifle weighed against her back and beads of sweat formed above her upper lip. Rebane waded through the knee-deep snow while the bigger cub pinned its sibling against the rocks and gnawed its ear. Then the duo parted to chase each other. Rebane ran after them, gesturing with her arms.

Her alarmed voice sounded like the quacking of a duck. "Come back! Your mother wants you to stay put! Otherwise, White Death won't find you when she returns from the hunt."

Both toy animals froze to look at the strange two-legged creature running toward them. The cubs looked baffled and cute beyond belief. Their fluff shone the purest of white in the early dawn, and the bigger cub tried to make sense of Rebane's species by smelling her scent. Rebane halted to recheck the darkened sea with her binoculars, but nothing signaled the presence of the mother polar bear.

They don't usually leave their cubs behind.

A plan dawned in her mind. Rebane opened her rucksack. With seal flesh in her hand, she called for the cubs. "Little beasts, come here. I have food."

The bigger one padded straight toward her and tried to steal the chunk of meat. Rebane lowered her hand onto the animal's back but the male cub didn't even flinch.

I'll bet you've never met a human before. We're a dangerous bunch, you know.

She ran her fingers through the white fluff and wild joy replaced her grief. Rebane couldn't stop herself from smiling. "I'll give you a potent Sami name, little boy. You are *Fámolaš—Strong—*because I know you'll grow up big and burly. You will eat many people and they won't be able to do anything about it."

Fámolaš replied by ripping loose a piece of yellow fat which hung by a tendon. As the silver hue predicted a new day, she kept an eye on *Fámolaš's* sibling. The smaller cub went around Rebane several times, each circle drawing closer. The female cub's body language revealed caution but the gaze in the beady bear eyes blinked with intelligence.

"You are *Muohta—Snow—*because of your beautiful fur," Rebane whispered into the breeze, which could translate her words into bear talk. She didn't move a muscle as *Muohta* stretched her neck to lick her finger.

Rebane remembered the scars which crisscrossed on White Death's snout. They reminded her of her own loose tooth and the notched rib—injuries from past battles with a powerful opponent. White Death must have beaten enormous males to claim this place as her kingdom.

White Death isn't an enemy. She's a mother—as I could have been.

The cubs lifted their alert heads before another roar of a fully grown beast echoed from the beach.

"Speak of the devil," Rebane gasped and her heart froze.

The pale morning had gained enough strength for Rebane to see the mother bear with her naked eye. White Death stood on her enormous hind paws a thousand feet to the left in the valley, sniffing the air for the human's scent. The beast's jug ears turned. Muohta leaned against Rebane's side and Fámolaš pushed his nose into her pocket.

Rebane had to push the cubs away before she sprang up and started running for her life. The moment she moved the polar predator began the chase. Muohta and Fámolaš mistook the hunt for a game and followed behind the human. Adrenaline spiked through her as Rebane realized she was between the mother and her cubs.

I'm so stupid!

Clouds of air exited from White Death's snout as the beast exhaled. The animal looked like a steam engine advancing with a sprinting speed of twenty-five miles per hour. The bear's gigantic paws extended into a gallop, and she clawed the air with twelve-inch blades as the ground shook under her weight. Rebane's heart thumped like a drum and she ignored the burn of lactic acid in her thighs. She ran as fast as she could, knowing White Death would cut her escape route in seconds.

I won't make it to the door!

With a pang of horror in her abdomen, she halted and drew the 9mm pistol from the belt holster. Rebane spread her legs and straightened her arms for a successful shot—her only chance. The bear grew enormous as the Sig's front and rear sights aligned in the middle of White Death's frost-white chest. Rebane's bowels knotted and she sucked in a breath she couldn't exhale. Her finger curled around the trigger as Muohta passed the human and padded downhill toward her mother. Fámolaš followed with clumsy gait, his furry bottom with the stub of a tail ridiculously bouncing up and down. Rebane lifted the barrel and the shot launched into the misty air above her head. The rock faces returned a muffled echo.

"I can't shoot you," she admitted in a defeated tone.

The mother bear stopped on her tracks with her ears pressed against her head. For a minute, the human and the blond bear measured each other.

"You recognize the sound. You've been shot at before," Rebane mumbled. The deep brown gaze of White Death reflected a strategic intellect.

The cubs danced around her their mother, rejoicing in their reunion. Fámolaš nibbled one of White Death's panda-like front paws, but Muohta crawled under her mother's belly and struggled to get to a teat. Rebane took the Tikka into her hands and released the rifle's safety button.

"You let me pass and I'll do the same for you," she whispered.

The polar bear's ears turned like a radar as the monster assessed the distance of the human with the firearm.

"Think of your cubs, White Death," Rebane added in a husky voice, but the beast answered only by touching her canine teeth with the tip of a pink bear tongue.

Rebane moved toward the entrance in hostile silence, the mama bear in her sights. The breeze cut through her pants and froze the tips of her exposed fingers. Her breath coming in short bursts, Rebane turned to unbolt the main door. Her hands shook as she looked over her shoulder. White Death remained in place, now rolled onto her back, and letting the cubs suckle with hungry force.

The tempest cried among the mountains like an old woman and Rebane understood why everyone had fled this place.

I know I'm not welcome here. The gorge is White Death's kingdom.

The Troll Mountain's grooves flooded with molten sunlight, now as red as blood in a wound. It was almost March. Spring waited behind the corner.

"I'll leave for Finland when the day temperature rises above minus eighteen degrees," Rebane said to herself as the iron door banged shut and the underground darkness devoured her.

19.
Container City—Part I

July 2049 in The Invisible Zone, formerly Finland.

The forest canopy moved above Rebane's head in the mellow wind. Even the crickets had returned to the Invisible Zone after two decades of extinction. Mosquito bites from last night itched on Rebane's ankles. Among the fresh grass and hot aromatic air, she smelled a whiff of the stalker, a man sweating in the scorch of July. The forest shuffled dark green and opened toward the sunlight. The group that had trailed her for miles stayed downwind on most occasions, but today one of them had drawn too near.

They're armed. Everyone here is.

The birch trees were young and spread out circa forty miles from the Container City—a rogue concentration of arms dealers and brothel owners. Ten years ago, when Rebane had joined the army, the land had sustained only conifers. This summer felt sweltering in a way she couldn't recall from a lifetime spent surviving under the ash clouds. She missed the ferocious wind which had bit her face as she'd crossed the frozen Gulf of Bothnia in April. May rushed by uneventful except for the two deserters who'd tried to kill her—or worse—while she scavenged an empty Russian missile base for lighter gear. June filled with stormy skies and swarms of newborn flies. Rebane spent her days soaking wet on foot and following the riverbeds of Ostrobothnia inland. But July spelled terrible news.

Comfortable weather means more people. Damn you, sun! You used to cower behind the clouds and let everything wither.

The coiled snake of the river would lead to her stepdad's cabin but she couldn't just settle there, not even if she was family. Rebane needed clearance from Mad Dog—the local warlord, who spoke only one language.

Violence.

A twig crushed under someone's boot. Rebane didn't mind the armed escort if they came from the Container City. She already had a plan regarding how to deal with Mad Dog but meeting the Russians would be an unlucky coincidence.

I don't want to kill men like my Daniil and loyal Ivanov. But on the other hand, I'd like to see that Russians still inhabit these latitudes.

Rebane hadn't come across a single Russian during her travels through the deserted midsection of Sweden. That wasn't a surprise since the radiation levels alternated between high and moderate depending on where clouds had rained cancer after the Stockholm blast. But no Russian forces in the fringes of the Zone—what used to be Finland—filled Rebane with icy dread. Mad Dog and the local Russian commander had a pact when she ran away from her stepdad's farm. The absence of Russia had everything to do with the cockiness in Weisser's voice. *We have learned to manufacture nukes again.* The dreadful echo had grown paler during the past ten months but still broke a cold sweat from Rebane's pores.

I have more pressing problems now.

Rebane traced a path she'd learned as a child who'd followed Pertti, her step-dad, on the hunt. The trail rose to high ground where she could take a look at the five men tailing her. The tank top beneath her camo shirt was glued moist against her back and Rebane yearned for a cold drink. She steadied herself through the steepest part of the climb by grabbing the trunks of the birches and crouching on the moss.

Fuck, the Tikka is heavy! There must be a rifle-shaped imprint on my back.

If the trackers belonged to Mad Dog's patrol, Rebane had crossed the buffer ring—a twenty-mile radius around the Container City.

No, I can't be that far off. The warlord's lair is sixty miles north.

As she reached the highest ledge, Rebane took a deep breath of the cooler air and whispered to herself, "The Russians have retreated, and Mad Dog has filled the power vacuum." She didn't dare think of with whom he might be in alliance nowadays.

If he struck a deal with the Union, I'm as good as dead.

She loosened the rucksack straps and laid the sniper rifle beside her. The mat of lichen felt soft against her belly. Biting her bottom lip, Rebane zoomed on what appeared to be the leader of the pack. He stood erect in the valley some two-hundred feet below and adjusted the visor of his cap to gaze in Rebane's direction. His skin was the color of terra cotta enhanced by the shadows of the forest moving in the warm breeze. Rebane noticed his square jaw, but the army green baseball cap hid most of his face. For a moment, the leader had caught her undivided attention. As he raised a muscular arm to signal the patrol to wait, she saw that black hair covered his forearms.

You're from the Middle East—a refugee.

The birdsong stopped before a cloud of sparrows startled into flight. They rode the thermal updraft into the white hot sky. The trail forced the patrol to form a successive chain, and Rebane could have sniped them one by one if she'd wanted. The second and third man remained under the canopy and she couldn't see them in detail. Rebane rotated the zoom ring of her binoculars. On the shoulder pad of the team leader's uniform shirt was the emblem of a grinning dog's skull.

Phew! Thank you, Fox Spirit—just shipping container dwellers.

"Hey, you!" he shouted. "The woman on top of the hill. You can come out now."

The underbrush rustled as Rebane rose to her feet. The man wiped the sweat from his brow but the index finger of his other hand never shifted from the trigger guard of his firearm. The call of a black-throated diver sounded. There had to be a lake or swamp nearby. Rebane kept her eyes on the leader as she secured her steps down the path. His military stance with a rigid back and open legs caused a surge of memory—warm and sore at the same time. She registered the hotness on her skin, but the leader's green-brown eyes studied her with sympathy.

"I'm Khaled," he said, introducing himself with a melodious voice. He offered a hand that Rebane shook without hesitation.

"Rebane," she replied, acutely aware of the rat's nest on top of her head and the dirt which coated her summer clothes. Khaled smiled as he said, "You can keep your rifle if you agree to come with us."

Surrounded by three more of Khaled's men armed and wearing desert-brown tactical vests, she nodded.

"Wait, I know her," The last man proclaimed from beyond the boulders. "She's my neighbor—or used to be."

His deep voice struck a familiar chord in Rebane, who snatched a sidelong glance. A local man with an amicable face and sun-striped beard emerged between the cattails. He leaned his plump hands against his knees and struggled to calm his breathing after the climb. He bore the distinct traits of the local guerrillas—dirty camouflage and outdated weapons—but he was too well-fed to belong to the resistance.

"Bjorn the rat," Rebane spat and stood upright as blood sang in her ears. Her hand crawled for the Sig's butt, but Khaled's dark brows knotted together. Rebane added, "And that's an insult to rats."

A pair of dimples softened the Finnish man's bulky face. "I know what Pertti Nordstrom said about me, but for the record, I always liked you, Reb." Bjorn's smile revealed a gold tooth in the front row.

"Don't speak of my father, informant!" she snapped. The tinder of the forest floor felt more flammable than ever before.

"If you two can travel in the same helicopter without starting a fight, I suggest we move to the plateau for our ride," Khaled suggested. Rebane hopped down the path without taking another look at Bjorn. Inside her chest, a storm brewed. The cloudless day could end in lightning and thunder.

Bloodshed.

The helicopter arrived in ten minutes, its rotator blades throwing turf and soil on Rebane's face. She had to wipe her tears on her sleeve several times before Khaled helped her step onboard. Bjorn sat opposite, but neither he nor Rebane looked at it each other during the uneventful flight.

I'll bet you've already sold my ass to Weisser—for a lot of money.

The Container City's main gate had been propped open for today's market of bullets and flesh, among other things. Before she could unbuckle her seat belt, another helicopter touched down on the asphalt helipad. The Union's circle of golden stars was painted across the hull of the Apache AH-64. She scanned the black uniforms of the two officers who stepped out while her heartbeat rumbled like a war drum. The taller man stood with his broad back toward her and Rebane tried to see if his sleeve pad depicted the logo of Military Intelligence. Mentally, she slid down a smooth, slippery slope toward hell.

The same cropped hair...and the same starched collar.

Rebane swallowed and her breath jammed in her throat. A feeling of utter loneliness intensified inside her. The man swayed, obviously drunk and trying to light his cigarette. Both officers turned to face Khaled's group and the other man succeeded in offering his lighter to the first one—who wasn't the devil. But the smoke from good Union tobacco still petrified Rebane into a scene in the past.

Someone squeezed her arm, startling her from her trance. Rebane saw the wisdom in Khaled's eyes which colored golden in the sunlight. He had registered her reaction and, without a word, seemed to signal *Don't worry. I'll protect you.* But Rebane's gaze repeatedly flitted toward the Union men. The duo entered the gates ahead of Khaled's team. She looked again to make sure the tall officer hadn't turned into the one she feared more than anything.

The Container City's wall was thirteen feet tall and consisted of rusty shipping containers stacked on top of each other. This tribe used them as building blocks for homes, as a line of defense, and as kiosks to distribute their illegal underage commodities. Nobody knew how the shipping containers ended on this marine graveyard a hundred miles inland. A ship's bow stood half-sunken into the ocean of grass a quarter mile from the citadel. Crazy legends about this place were widespread among the scattered locals. On both sides of the gate, two manned posts towered with machine gun turrets. A pair of rusted-through Toyota pickups stood guard with mobile missile pads mounted on their pallets.

Nukes?

The silhouettes of the warheads appeared menacing against the sky. Harbingers of thin clouds predicted a bright, hot afternoon. A movement drew Rebane's attention—a man wearing the ragged remnants of a power suit trampled circles into the waving grass. He squeezed the handle of a leather suitcase as if his life depended on it.

"Don't mind Anderson," Khaled said as he turned to look at Rebane. "He's harmless. Some people were unable to handle the apocalypse."

"I know," Rebane replied. Her sense of foreboding intensified as the stream of people flowed through the gates. Sweaty bodies of mercenaries and courtesans pressed against her sides. Rebane's skin tingled, but everyone else seemed to be in a festive mood.

Khaled waited until she caught up with him. His eyes squinted into lines as he smiled. "But if you'd like some advice on your stock market portfolio, Anderson is your man." Rebane released a burst of nervous laughter. The sun created a softness which enhanced the crazy man's silhouette before the containers blocked him from Rebane's view.

"Stay close to me," Khaled suggested. His soldiers formed a line after Rebane. The radios strapped on their shoulders chattered.

Music pounded from the clubs and brothels. Rebane smelled roasted meat mixed with sweat and other secretions of the human body. The shipping containers emanated the odor of heated metal in the sun. She locked eyes with a madame who leaned her shoulder against the doorway of her establishment. The woman patted the dust from a floral dressing gown that had seen better days. Two of her employees crouched under a pentice to heat crack cocaine. The younger one wore fishnet stockings under denim shorts. Despite the punk hairdo that defied gravity, she couldn't be older than twelve.

"We sell every vice on earth," proclaimed the sign above the Madame's head. It made Rebane retch. A hand landed on her shoulder, as heavy as a meat hook. She turned to stare daggers at the perpetrator. It was Bjorn.

"Good to be home," Bjorn started, and Rebane hoped that he didn't notice how his touch had made her jump.

You expect them to hand you the grand prize? Wait and see. The Container people don't fancy squealers like you.

"If you like your fingers attached to your hand, don't touch me." Rebane ran her tongue across the sharpness of her upper teeth.

"You know they tortured me in the Union outpost, don't you?" Bjorn asked, but Rebane had already hurried on so as not to lose sight of Khaled and his men.

She collected her nerve when the convoy reached the central square lined with vegetable stands, tattoo parlors and the organized shop fronts of the Container City's legendary gunsmiths. Atop a rusty container which spelled in man-sized all caps *CHINA SHIPPING*, rested a ripped-up armchair. In its plush embrace sat the Mad Dog—a corpulent man with a bald head wearing a leather vest and pirated copy of Levi's jeans. Two of his beefy lieutenants stood guard, armed to the teeth.

Ya'laa, a tall African woman, sat on the armrest of Dog's throne and wiggled her perfect toes in sandals. A myriad of colors sparkled each time the sun hit the rhinestones of the leather straps. She held her chin high at the end of a royal neck. This was the Queen of Container City, whose enticing beauty—and business instincts—had made her a star. Everyone knew Ya'laa's story, from a sex slave to the richest female in the Zone. Beneath the incredibly long lashes, her coal-black eyes narrowed to measure Rebane like livestock in a country fair. Ya'laa tilted her head and her hanging diamond earrings brushed skin that was smooth and made of dark silk. Rebane stared back at her.

If I can't take my eyes off you, no wonder you've driven men to madness and suicide—the victims of Ya'laa, frequent as grains of sand.

But the captain of the patrol never even glanced at Ya'laa. Khaled and Rebane stood shoulder-to-shoulder. The sun hammered at her, hotter than an anvil. Khaled was a head taller and had to bow to whisper in her ear. "Fight dirty and keep your eyes on me." She felt the warmth of his breath on her cheek. "I know you can do it, and no one will be able to touch you after you win." Khaled ran his fingers through his hair and adjusted the Yankees baseball cap perched on top of his head.

The Queen shifted her long legs and bent to whisper into Mad Dog's cauliflower ear. Rebane could almost hear how the gold bracelets jingled on the Somali woman's wrists and the silk dress ruffled against the body of a professional dancer. Mad Dog put his shovel hand on the butt of the Smith & Wesson .357 in his belt. One of the courtiers, a redhead with freckled skin and nervous manner, climbed the ladder to the podium carrying a megaphone.

After the initial high-pitched interference, Mad Dog looked down and rumbled, "State your name, woman."

Rebane tugged at her cargo pants and replied in a confident voice, "Rebane Nordstrom."

A hush traveled through the crowd, where people stood like salted herrings in a tin can. A hundred eyes focused on her, making Rebane feel alone and naked. In the tightly packed crowd that a mouse couldn't fit through, a stocky grandma elbowed her way to the front row. She tapped Rebane on the shoulder and handed her a piece of paper. Rebane smoothed the print. From it, her prison mug photo stared back at her. The grandma pointed at the text with a blackened fingernail and winked. Five languages boasted that the spy was worth 200,000 euros alive. A twinge of fear twisted Rebane's entrails. Men lifted their kids onto their shoulders and the bookies were already at it. Rebane heard how people argued about her fate. An old woman offered a pig as a bet for the spy's extradition and the animal oinked in protest.

Mad Dog cleared his throat before the megaphone blasted his order. "Make room for her, people. We're not savages!" A clearing formed around Rebane, only to shrink again. "You are wanted for the murder of the President of the European Union."

Rebane swallowed the lump in her throat. Her fist closed around the strap of the Tikka. The rifle's metal felt like lava between her shoulder blades.

The Dog continued. "I might add that the GRU offered less than half for your severed head, but the Russians left with their tails between their legs." The crowd roared with laughter. Ya'laa threw her arms in the air and her breasts bounced with the movement. A stream of jet-black braids flowed down her shoulders as she snatched the loudspeaker.

"Well, Rebane. Are you familiar with the rules of this place?" Ya'laa purred into the mouthpiece and offered a bold smile with astonishing teeth.

Everybody knows you can fight your way out of any trouble here.

"Yes," Rebane answered, louder than she intended. "I'll fight whomever you want, noble Queen." A chilly shudder went through her despite the July sunshine.

As the crowd roared and whistled, Rebane scanned the faces for the Union officers, but she only saw the eccentric warriors and punksters of the citadel and the soot-painted faces of the hunter-gatherers who'd happened to stumble to the market today.

I hope a brothel has swallowed your drunken asses and the girls smother you with their pillows while you sleep!

Ya'laa's eyes filled with fire as she shouted, "Let the betting begin! You know whom she must fight."

Great. I'm the only one who doesn't know.

While the locals struggled to join the wave surging in front of the betting kiosks, Rebane saw Bjorn, who loomed taller than most people. Their eyes met and she knew he predicted doom. He elbowed and plowed others with his plump body until he got near enough to speak to her.

"You're crazy," he said in a woolly voice, his face sweaty and pink. "Your opponent is even bigger than me." A smell of tobacco and chicory coffee wafted from Bjorn, and Rebane remembered why she hated people who smoked.

"You have guts, Reb, but I just placed all my money on *him*."

"Good for you, rat," she spat through clenched teeth. "I'll make sure you lose every bloodstained nickel."

But inside, her breath stopped, and her heart sank.

Fuck! What have I done?

20.
Container City—Part II

A boy perhaps seven years of age sold local brews of liquor and moonshine by the jarful. He had harnessed a black Labrador to draw the booze cart and its tail beat against the slats like a baton. Bare-kneed and wearing a blue T-shirt which depicted a cartoon polar bear, he stood in front of Rebane holding a dipper of cloud-colored moonshine.

"For courage, Miss," he said in Russian. "It's free because Papa says you're faster than the Bull."

The Bull? That can't be good.

Rebane drew back her head and drained the alcohol in one mouthful. "Thanks, little fellow," she said, but the boy had already yelled, "Mush!" and the black dog had moved twenty feet forward with a lazy jog.

Khaled's men formed a chain and forced people to make room for the fighters. Rebane remained standing alone in the middle of the clearing with a lump the size of a tennis ball in her throat. The grandma had bought a grilled rib from the butcher's shop and ate with smacking noises but Rebane felt like throwing up. She tried to formulate a sequence of fighting moves but her brain drew a blank. Her palms sweated and her mouth tasted like dirt despite the moonshine burning her intestines.

"The betting has closed." The announcement interrupted her self-pitying. "Ladies and gentlemen, make room for the Bull!" Mad Dog yelled.

Khaled materialized beside Rebane. He looked thoughtfully into the distance before he faced her. "You must give up your weapons. It's a knuckle-to-knuckle fight," he said in a colorless tone which couldn't hide his worry. Seagulls called above their heads.

"Can I keep my knife?" Rebane asked as she lifted the rifle strap over her head and handed the Tikka to him. She braided her hair with quick fingers to keep the loose strands off her face at a crucial moment. The wind had picked up and slammed the windowpanes of a container home.

I need to pee so bad.

"Captain Karasholi," the voice of the loudspeaker addressed. "To ensure fair betting, please search the challenger for hidden weapons."

"No need for that," Rebane shouted back, parting with the Sig and the hunting knife. From the podium, Ya'laa flashed one of her shining smiles before she took another sip of red wine.

A hush traveled through the crowd. It became so quiet that Rebane could hear her breath. Someone's head and shoulders bobbed above the waves of people. A bearded man with the physique of a beef ox took his place opposite Rebane. This professional wrestler had to be thrice her size! He ripped his shirt in half with a grunt and threw the pieces to the giggling farm girls nearby. The Bull's chest was like a cognac barrel and his tribal-tattooed biceps thicker than both of Rebane's thighs pressed together. She stood rooted to the spot and her jaw dropped.

"I'll snap your neck like a carrot," the Bull threatened. Furrows appeared between his brows and someone whistled at full force.

For Mielikki's sake! I can't beat him. Not without a gun.

Rebane staggered back, unsure of her steps.

Then the Bull exploded into hearty laughter and slapped Rebane on top of her head. She landed on her butt in the hot sand, scorching red with humiliation.

"I can't fight her," the strongman yelled toward the podium. From behind, his shorts struggled to stretch around his enormous buttocks. "She's a little girl," he objected.

Rebane rose to her feet and knotted her shirt around her waist by the sleeves.

I'll show you what this little girl can do.

"What the fuck?" Mad Dog bellowed through the crackling microphone. "You know the rules, Bull. You fight the woman until either one of you is dead—unless the crowd wants to pardon the loser."

Bull's scream of agony sliced the argument. Rebane attacked with a fast cut from behind with her hidden knife and went for his ankle. Blood oozed from the wound into his car-sized shoe and his face grimaced with pain. He turned on all fours and his gorilla-like arms reached for her. She backed up with the knife in a reverse grip.

You should have patted me down, Khaled.

Rebane knew she hadn't used enough force to sever his tendon. When the Bull straightened his massive body her head rushed with adrenaline.

"You little fuck!" he cursed and charged with a dust cloud rising behind him.

Running for her life, Rebane followed the edges of the opening in the crowd. She gained enough distance to face the raging Bull and estimate his direction. With a straight back and lowered arms, she moved to the side. This dodge was the most straightforward movement in the Systema book. Rebane's head cleared and she executed the next movement from well-rehearsed muscle memory. As the mountain of flesh swooshed by, she turned and plunged the rubber-grip blade into the side of his waist. The Bull staggered forward, driven by his mass and force. But the wound only made him madder.

"Why can't you stay down?" she screamed as the Bull removed the knife from his meat and let out animal noises. He balanced the blade in his left hand and bared his teeth at Rebane.

"Come kitty, kitty," he teased and switched hands. He didn't even notice the blood running from the wound between his ribs.

Rebane let him come near enough to strike once. The steel blade cut through her trouser leg, brushing her shin with the serrating edge, and causing sharp pain. The Bull grabbed her braid and yanked her head back. They stared at each other wild-eyed while the beast breathed cheese and old booze on her. Rebane squeezed the giant's knife-holding hand—her fingers didn't even meet around his wrist—and side-kicked him twice. The sunlight reflected from the steel. In a frenzy, she bit, scratched, delivered a series of fast left kicks into his ribs, and drew tufts of curly hair from his scalp.

Nothing worked. The crowd bellowed. It sounded like the roar of waves coming through deep water. Bathed in sweat, she knew the Bull would stab her to death. Then a thought occurred to her.

Anger coursed through Rebane's veins, but she mimicked a high-pitched voice to plead, "Let me go, please." She breathed fast through her teeth and looked into the deep-seated eyes of her opponent.

"Okay, baby rabbit." Bull's face melted into a victory smile, just inches from her face. "Let's give the audience a show for their money."

As he let go of her hair, she ran crisscrossing into the crowd. He stopped to take a bow and kiss a girl on the mouth.

What a show-off.

Rebane picked up stones and hurled them at him. She used apples from the fruit stand. She even snatched a high-heeled shoe from a prostitute and threw it at the wrestler's face. All this amused him—and the spectators.

"Now, your time is up, bitch," Bull snarled. "I'll strangle your lights out and use you like a mattress."

This time, Rebane didn't run. She couldn't keep herself from smiling. She stood precisely where Khaled's eyes had guided her five minutes ago, next to a skinny man well past his seventies and with the white hair of an ostrich of top of his head. He jumped up and down with his arms in the air.

On his belt was a leather holster with a strap missing a button. Rebane grabbed the handle of the old revolver in a simple, smooth move. She enjoyed the sound of the cocking hammer and took a fighting stance with flexed knees. Her left hand steadied the right, forming a seamless hold around the butt grip. Clutching the gun, Rebane exhaled the breath she had been holding.

Dizziness engulfed her and the crowd disappeared into a haze. But the man in front of her, his ugly features remained clear and detailed. The Bull stared into the barrel zeroing in on his chest. A stream of sweat made its way down between his bulging pectoral muscles. He held the knife in his hand but seemed unable to decide whether he should run or charge. Rebane squeezed the trigger with complete follow-through. The gun sent out a 38 Special with massive recoil and cloud of gunpowder. The explosion banged her ears from close range and echoed between the containers. She knelt on the hot ground and spat a trail of saliva and blood. The .38 remained in her lap.

When she raised her eyes, Rebane saw Ya'laa bouncing up and down on the podium. She screamed into the loudspeaker, "Yes! Finally." The Bull stayed down, deceased. A thunderstorm of applause and catcalls rose from the audience. Mad Dog rolled his eyes. The man whose gun Rebane had snatched shook his bony fist and objected, "The bitch cheated. She stole my revolver."

He received a slap on the face from a stocky woman with a baby in her arms. "Shut your mouth, old goat," she yelled with flushed, chubby cheeks. "The Russian won fair and square—against a superior opponent. Who says you can't use what's here? Now give me my money!"

In the shade of Ya'laa's container, a medic bandaged Rebane's shin. The Somali goddess stretched out on a pile of red velvet pillows and waited for an answer. The ceiling fan provided a stream of air which Rebane desperately needed to clear her head. She splashed ice water from a bucket onto her face and watched it replacing the dirt on its way across her chest. Rebane's neck hurt but she met the black night of Ya'laa's eyes and said, "I have enough blood on my hands. I can't ask your people to die for me."

"You knew we were in alliance with the reds?" the African asked in an innocent tone.

"Yes. I used to be one of them," Rebane said, clearing her throat.

"Then you must understand that the Union has a beef with us no matter what you do?"

Rebane hesitated but decide to spit it out. "Maybe striking a deal with them would be a good idea, under the circumstances."

"We have nukes."

Rebane shifted her dusty boot. Her socks were soaking wet and needed a laundering. The scented goddess made her feel secondhand. After a sigh, Rebane said, "No. I must leave so you can stay impartial."

A long finger lifted Rebane's chin, and the woman's bracelets jingled. Ya'laa had moved across the floor without a sound. "Do you think you're the only wanted person here? We've been around since the Apocalypse because we take in refugees and because we sell everything for everyone. This is the fringe of the world. When the cold returns, the Union will forget about us. The way the frivolous weather is, it could happen tomorrow."

"True," Rebane admitted and let out an *ouch* as she rubbed her sore neck.

Ya'laa studied her with a knowing smile on her painted lips. Rebane couldn't get over the symmetry of the Queen's features and feared she would drown in the dark sea that was Ya'laa.

"You know how many men have sent assassins after me?" Ya'laa's eyes grew dreamy as she rolled a joint. Her lashes curtained her gaze.

Rebane didn't answer. The fight had gone out of her.

"Well, I've lost count. As will you," the Queen whispered and inhaled from her joint. "Follow captain Karasholi on an expedition and then decide if you want to leave. This place can offer a lot to a skilled sniper."

Rebane couldn't resist the temptation. "If that means little boys, I'll skip." As Ya'laa's expression grew cunning, Rebane added, "I meant no offense..."

Mischief flashed in her eyes. "I'll tell you a secret. I wasn't born in Africa. My great grandparents came to Finland long before the war. I'm as much a local as you."

"Then why the legends?"

"A girl has to take care of her brand!"

The peculiar smell of marijuana bothered Rebane. Ya'laa fingered her rings and studied the diamonds with an expert gaze. "You are around thirty?" She asked and didn't pause for Rebane's reply. "You should secure your future. Maybe choose one of our pregnant women? A special product, the mothers were born after the cataclysm and are guaranteed to be fertile."

Rebane thought about being pregnant.

Who wants to bring a child into this world?

But she chose not to offend her benefactor again. "No, thanks. I can hardly sustain myself."

Her answer didn't deter the saleswoman. "For a special price, a doctor from the Union airbase can combine your eggs with the semen of a strong man."

The man I want is dead, Rebane thought, but asked, "Is there any place you can't reach?"

There it was again—Ya'laa's enigmatic smile. Her silk dress folded like the wind bent a wheat field. "Promise me you'll think about staying here," Ya'laa suggested as she crushed the stump of the joint under her sandal and rose to leave. On the doorstep, she turned to look at Rebane. "Your cabin isn't far enough away for safety."

"I know. And I'm thankful for the Queen's concern," Rebane whispered. "But I must find my dad."

Ya'laa threw her head back and laughed. "Stay here. We're armed to the teeth. If the Union wants a piece of you, they'll have to come through us."

PART III

21.
Ground Zero

A young moon lay on its back among the ragged clouds. It was still dark when the Sisu Defence truck halted in the outer zone of the blast radius. The scouts jumped off the *ass*—military slang for an armored vehicle—to check the perimeter. Everyone used the respite however they saw fit. Rebane visited the towering willows for a pee. An approaching storm charged the air. The smell of damp earth lingered when the dawn arrived cold and windy.

When the scouts returned, their leader, with a sunburned face and a ridiculous mustache, saluted Khaled and gave him a report. "All clear within the inner perimeter, sir. The first outpost appears deserted. The gates have been busted open. Maybe a feud between the locals? But we heard faraway gunshots which we couldn't locate."

"At ease," captain Karasholi replied. A standard mission brief followed. "The operational conditions look calm, but the zombies have tricked us before. Watch out for tripwires and pit traps."

Everyone answered with one voice. "Yes, captain."

"You keep whatever you find," the second in command, a Finnish man in camouflage and combat boots, shouted. Many of the men were veterans from Russian or Union troops. The latter type bothered Rebane most. She feared Bjorn wasn't alone.

Khaled stared at Rebane with intense eyes. "Second Lieutenant Nordstrom will search for a suitable location. She will snipe if we bump heads with the locals. I'll be her pair." The rugged features of this man at war whipped up memories she wanted to keep below the surface and the mention of her military rank tinged with sorrowful irony. She removed her tactical glove to run a finger along the smooth surface of the Tikka's silencer. She felt the captain's eyes on her as she maintained the bearing of her military days.

Don't grow too fond of him. Tomorrow brings violence and heartbreak.

The team continued on foot. The two Russians tried to amuse her by telling dirty jokes and accompanying them with barking laughter. Rebane answered with a chuckle out of polite habit. They passed a stripped-down cellular tower which leaned against the shoulder of a house. It was late July but the weather had turned and reminded her of the middle of September. Oppressive silence accompanied

Khaled and Rebane as the patrol divided into reconnaissance duos. The wind moaned between the buildings. Not even the V-formation of geese flying above their heads could ease her nervousness.

Someone had already rummaged through the intestines of suburban homes and tossed melted kitchen utensils and scorched bricks outside. Rebane's hair flew in the air and the fabric of a torn trampoline fluttered. The blast wave had shattered every window. Rebane almost expected the sunken face of a ghost child to peek out from between the checkered curtains which the wind rustled.

The spirits of the dead can snatch your soul. That's what Khadne used to say.

Rebane spied from the corner of her eye how Khaled buried his chin inside the camouflage muffler. The assault rifle with the extra-large magazine and a new laser pointer rested against his tactical vest. Rebane's stomach sank as the breeze raised dust in the major-damage-reparable zone but her dosimeter never sounded an alarm. She touched the small lines around her slanted eyes. Her skin yearned for moisture.

When I get home I must make an ointment from wild honey and nettle. Maybe the rye already grows their small ears of grain on Papa's fields.

She followed Khaled onto an overpass and felt a tingling of alarm as if a predator were watching her. High pillars, legs of a dinosaur, supported the bridge in midair. Where the curve of another freeway disappeared into a grey-blue mist, a flash caught her eye. Reflexively, she rammed into Khaled and yelled, "Duck!" But only a rust-eaten road sign squeaked as it hung from a bent metal bar above their heads.

"Where?" he asked.

"I saw a reflection by the collapsed lane," she said in a tight tone. "Cover me. I'll take a look. And ask the B- or C-team to wait for location coordinates. Which one is closer to us?"

Khaled rapped into his radio, "Team Beta, a possible backbiter at two o'clock. Phantom-Shadow-Celsius. Please confirm and stand by. Over and out."

"Yes, sir," the radio buzzed. "Beta affirmative." A bit later, team C echoed the same.

Rebane crawled on her belly to a spot where blocks from the median barrier had crumbled. She removed her wool beanie and opened the bipod for a steady long-distance shot. Adjusting the zoom ring of the Tikka's scope to 10X, she browsed the smoke-licked walls. The iron bars from steel concrete protruded against the clouded sky like ribs of a whale. Nothing caught her eye.

Fear makes you see things that aren't going to jump at you.

But the attack arrived soundlessly as a bullet blasted dust to the right of her. She flattened before the enemy sniper hit closer with his second approach.

"Khaled?" she shouted.

"Probably out of my range," he yelled. Rebane rolled to a different position. The third shot arrived above Khaled's spot and allowed her to see the muzzle flash from the first-floor window of a garage—and the heat of the fourth bullet in flight.

"Position?" he called and flattened.

"By the detonation crater. A three-story garage with broken ramps, on the first-floor window opening on the left, I think—unless he moved." Sweat sprung from her pores. She drew breath through clenched teeth.

"Sector Beta-45-9," Khaled screamed into the radio. "Sarah-Gamma!!" Within five seconds, the B-team released a smokescreen and directed random fire toward the garage. Grenade launchers fired large-caliber projectiles, but Rebane couldn't tell if gas warheads rained on the sniper among the smoke. Whatever it was, it forced the man to run.

She pushed the lever of the bolt lock, feeding a .308 into the chamber. Rebane drew the recoil pad of the butt against her pectoral muscle and waited until a whirlwind lifted the smokescreen. The sniper was a freckle-faced young man. He dashed across the street with agile legs. Rebane aimed at the bulk of him, not knowing if he wore body armor under his anorak. She fired too soon—without proper advance—and missed as he dived for cover. The young man blended among the rubble with his city-camo outfit but there were of blood drops on the tarmac.

"You wounded him," Khaled said.

"I know, but a sniper is seldom alone. Call for a helicopter from the Container City sir."

"It will take 30 minutes for air support to arrive."

"We'd better make our way to high ground, then," Rebane said under her breath. She stayed low behind the cover of the median barrier. She turned to look at Khaled, who ended the radio transmission. "Let's move, Captain Karasholi. We don't have much time if the zombie boy has friends."

"I ordered the B and C to do a sweep." As confirmation, a burst of automatic fire sounded far away. A raven dived out of the clouds, circling above Rebane's head and cawing.

Khaled jumped across the hole in the asphalt and bumped into Rebane. His gaze swept over the bird. "Some say the raven is an omen of war."

Rebane's heart thumped. "There's always a war. That's what humans do—kill."

"An odd thing for a sniper to say." His breathing quickened as she looked at him.

"Please don't tell me you shoot ravens because they mean evil," he said.

Rebane's anger flared, but then she noticed the sparkle in his amber eyes. "I've never shot an animal I didn't intend to eat."

Khaled laughed.

"And ravens don't taste good. I hope you like the taste of a roasted zombie. Now run!" Rebane sprinted to the end of the freeway curve and landed with flexed knees on the ground three feet below.

Smoke from another explosion belched into the sky but the rat-a-tat of assault rifles soon ceased. Crouching and crawling from cover to cover, the duo advanced toward the only standing structure on the verge of the detonation crater. The hull of the garage towered in front of them, its walls battered by projectile material from the nuclear blast. Khaled appeared bulky in his gear but moved quickly up the stairs. Rebane hopped two or three stairs at a time but couldn't catch him.

To her relief, the place was empty. On the roof, she saw Khaled shading his eyes against the leaded sunlight. He leaned back against the wall of the elevator shaft. The bullet holes in the stone revealed that people had fought for whatever this Godforsaken graveyard could offer.

Rebane's careful peek at the horizon revealed a river in the distance, its waters glimmering behind a shroud of mist. Dust devils danced among the rubble. Above their heads, the clouds marched with terrible speed.

Maybe I missed my shot because of the wind speed? It creates a tunnel in tight spaces.

They wormed their way to the southern edge on their bellies. Rebane glanced at Khaled's severe face, his mouth a tight, determined line. With inner trembling, she waited for an enemy bullet to hit her flesh. She listened for the muffled tap of a sniper's rifle, but only the wind brushed the ruins. The fall had to be thirty feet, and the twisted steel railing groaned in the wind. Despite her fear of heights, Rebane lay on the ledge among loose bricks and let Khaled place his hand on the small of her back.

I wish I'd worn a helmet.

Ground Zero was a burrowed crater in the middle of something that had once been a square. Everything—the government buildings and shopping centers—had been vaporized. A pond of glassy substance shone green at the bottom of a hole a hundred feet deep. Rebane's rubber-lined pair of gloves provided a good grip, but the sheer immensity of the landscape created dizzying vertigo. She focused the Tikka's crosshairs on the low ground and felt herself redden as Khaled's eyes measured her.

"The falcon?" he inquired on the radio, which crackled an answer. "Minus ten minutes, and the delivery package contains presents for the birthday girl."

"Heat-guided missiles," Khaled explained.

That's when Rebane located Team Beta, huddling in position behind a set of concrete slabs. When the team leader rose and signaled the advance with his arm, Rebane saw the bubble of heat—the signature of the sniper's bullet—before the leader's stomach burst open. The Container man folded with a surprised expression on his face. His mouth gaped at the sight of his guts spilling out from the rupture. Rebane watched how he lay in agony, taking ragged breaths before another shower of smoke and gas poured from Team Beta.

When the young sniper moved his wounded leg and took another Beta into his sights, Rebane saw him. He lay prone like a starfish. The A-bomb had lifted ground as the blast wave traveled outward. A man-sized groove hid the Zombie, who blended into the terrain with exquisite detail. The flapping of the helicopter's rotor blades approached beyond the horizon and sent the ravens croaking. A gentle breeze swept across Rebane's face, and she suppressed a shiver.

"I'll take that backbiter down now," she huffed to Khaled. "Tell me where I hit in case I miss."

"Affirmative."

In her crosshairs some four-hundred feet away lay the enemy sharpshooter, magnified through the reticle of her scope. He had no idea that someone high above had him in her sights. She aimed at his spine but decided to move up a notch.

Goodbye, she thought before the rubber-lined surface of her shooting glove pressed against the trigger.

Rebane impaled the youngster with her .308 hollow-point. His head jerked like a jack-in-the-box as she severed his skull from the spine. Relief flooded her. She leaned her forehead against the rifle's stock and felt as if she couldn't breathe. With naked eyes, she watched the helicopter launch a rocket with an evil swoosh. Rebane had just enough time to cover her ears before the fireball licked the sky that turned soot black. The blast wave broke against the garage, rocking the roof under her belly. Rebane wanted to curl into a ball.

Khaled's grip on her shoulder was almost bruising. "Great accuracy, and without the help of a good spotter. You're GRU-trained, aren't you?" The nearness of his body caused the tips of her ears to burn. Or maybe it was the heat rising from the inferno.

"I used to be," she replied in a clipped military voice.

Now I'm just a deserter who gets to stick her head through the noose.

The Tikka's safety button clicked on and another tremor went through her. Rebane took a second look at the Zombie, but the blast had vaporized him. She tried to swallow but her throat was dry. The sniper's blue eyes had been full of fire as he'd dashed for cover—he couldn't have been older than twenty. On her feet, Rebane gaped at the chrome-colored sun emerging from the clouds.

"I'm glad you're on our side," Khaled commented, the wind flapping his fatigues.

"Am I," Rebane blurted, "on your side?" She regretted it immediately. She opened the zipper of her camouflage jacket. The northern wind streamed under her clothes. Grey flakes danced in the air, and she extended her free hand to catch a few.

Ash.

"Sweep clear," the radio on his shoulder strap echoed. "Falcon waits for the birthday party. Landing pad Gamma-4." Rebane noticed the handgun in a leg holster on the captain's thigh.

A gorgeous Sig P365 Nitron Micro-Compact. I'd kill for a 9mm like that.

"Do you want my spy to find out?" Khaled asked with a direct gaze. His expression grew stern.

"Find what out?"

"If the man you fear is in the Union airbase. They have a new commander."

A jolt went through her like a surprise lightning strike from a clear sky. "Who told you about Major Weisser? That fucker Bjorn?" Rebane wanted to vomit.

"I never heard the mention of his name but thank you for trusting me enough to share that information."

Rebane bit her bottom lip.

You should have kept your mouth shut!

Khaled's hand brushed her temple in a gentle gesture. The smile made him look ten years younger. "Why do you always assume someone ratted you out? I observe and notice things—especially when I like the person I'm looking at." He tugged at his ear protruding from under his beanie.

"Yes, I'd like to know who runs the base, just in case..." Rebane managed to say. "By the way, can the helicopter pilot do a detour and take me halfway to the western bog?"

"Sure," Khaled replied, masking his disappointment.

"It's just something I must do," she said, her voice desperately weary. "It doesn't mean that we won't see each other again." She hated herself that she'd given him hope.

"You'd be safer in the Container City with me." Khaled tried once more. "I'll make sure you get anything you want, even the P365 Nitron, you have your eyes on—unless you were measuring my thigh muscles."

"I owe it to him," she added without looking at him. Rebane shifted her boots and stirred dust.

"Your husband?"

"No, silly," she laughed. "Pertti Nordstrom. My dad."

Khaled let out a breath of relief. "You scared me there, Reb."

The sun had become a powerless glow behind the radio masts of what might have been a teleoperator's main office. A crumbling satellite dish dangled from a balcony, defying gravity. A bumblebee insisted on buzzing around Khaled's head and Rebane chased it away. Khaled was forty-five. Hair grew silver at his temples, but his body was trim and muscular. Rebane had to admit she liked what she saw.

Of all the people I know, I want to hurt you the least. And that's why I must go.

The clouds were white against the ash-colored sky and she thought of embracing him. "Perhaps we should head back to the rendezvous point," Rebane suggested instead. She felt the approaching tempest in the root of her broken tooth. The icy dread lurked below her conscious mind, drifting like the fog among the dense foliage—the eyes of darkness ever watchful for a mistake on her part.

It's time to hide and never come out again.

22.
Hunter's Moon

Rebane padded to the bedroom in her socks and wearing Papa's woolly sweater which smelled of grass. She avoided the pale stranger in the polished metal of the mirror. Her headache had become so intense today that she'd vomited three times after breakfast. The pain in her kidneys reminded her to kneel, not bow, to get the moonshine. Rebane opened the twin doors of the cupboard and the hinge let out a mournful screech. Twelve jars of clouded homemade alcohol stood in neat rows just as Pertti's hand had arranged them yesterday. Wiping away the cobwebs, she sent their architects running for the darkest corners. She took the first jar from the left, opening the lid with careful fingers.

I'm an unholy soldier without a country or a cause. My time is up.

Rebane's trek across the treacherous bog had woken a choir of frogs. The earth turned coffee grounds brown from unceasing rain, the mud sucking on Rebane's boots with every step. No one else knew the secluded pathway that led to the house and she didn't bother looking for a detour.

It will take a lot more than a bolt hole in the bog to save my life.

But when she laid eyes on the tall weeds which had conquered the yard, she immediately knew Pertti didn't live there anymore. The landfill behind the old log cabin had turned to earth a long time ago. The wild oats shuffled in the wind, uncut, moss growing on the roof shingles. A raccoon dog nested inside the groundwork. And now Rebane was too ill to leave.

The weeks lingered on while her hope faded. The timber building startled Rebane with bangs and creaks. By the kitchen table, sitting in Papa's chair, she let the alcohol descend as fire into her empty stomach.

At least it numbs the headache and the muscle pain.

Rain lashed at the windows, wasting the fury of the storm. A crack in the ceiling released a drop into the bucket, then another, and the sound of running water became the sleep medicine she needed. With her cheek resting against her elbow, Rebane dreamt restlessly. The Tikka rifle lay on the desk, never out of reach.

When she woke when it was dark outside, and she rushed to the bucket in the corner before vomit expelled in a violent arc. With cast iron legs, Rebane returned to the kitchen chair and swallowed the next gagging. A dim light from the oil lamp cast shadows over the walls but she was too exhausted to unite a lit match with the birch bark in the fireplace.

Shit! It's getting worse. I haven't healed at all.

She wiped the moist windowpane with her sleeve in order to gaze to the yard where the grass was rimed with frost. The hunter's moon gazed in through the half-closed curtains. She blew her running nose on a rag that smelled of Dad's machine oil, green-yellow mucus expelling with a hacking cough that bent Rebane double. When she could breathe again, she put her elbows on her table and prayed to the Goddess of the forest.

> *Mielikki, lady of the woods,*
> *queen of the wilderness!*
> *You caused my sores, now grant the cure*
> *Take the devil from me.*
> *There is your home,*
> *beyond the great bank, in the darkness of the north,*
> *in the mossy morass,*
> *in the sparkling spring.*
> *I took water from the spring,*
> *Now cleanse me from the evil, wash me clean from my sores.* ³

The can slipped to the floor with a racket that could wake the dead. Rebane jolted upright as the screws and nails scattered on the hardwood floor—someone had stepped on the steel tripwire running across the rye field.

"Not now." The knowledge of the impending attack cut through her mind like a razor blade. "I'm too sick to defend the place."

The second can upset, which meant the gravel road. Rebane had seven minutes to get out. She killed the light, buttoned Pertti's raincoat and laced her combat boots up to her shins. Grabbing the Tikka, she made her rehearsed moves without any noise. She opened the bedroom window and held her breath as the old window frame whined. From the kitchen came the sound of the last can crashing to the floor. She lowered the dispatch rucksack, always packed and ready, to the moist grass mat outside. Grunting, Rebane squirmed out of the window and landed feet first in the dark. She crossed the ninety feet of lawn to the pothole under the blackberry bushes and glanced at the house. In the stark moon's light, the cabin appeared as desolate as on the day she'd returned.

But I forgot the bucket. The vomit is fresh!

She squeezed her teeth shut, lifting the lid. Several layers of grass knotted onto a wooden frame, meshing the pit entrance with the foliage. The cover could stand the weight of a grown man. Taking a deep breath, she descended into the hole and filled her lungs with the damp air of the bog. The bottom felt mushy under her hands and she tried not to think about the insects that might crawl into her hair.

Sitting on the ammo crate, Rebane took out the night-vision goggles Khaled had given her from her rucksack. Gaping the lid a few inches more, Rebane perceived two silhouettes on the gravel road, sailing from side to side because they dragged something putting up a fight. The gravel rattled under their feet. Drops of sweat formed above Rebane's upper lip. Her breath misted in the moonlight.

A burst of muffled laughter followed. "Where's the light? Kurt, bring the light!" A broad-shouldered man with branches attached to his helmet stood on her porch stairs. He turned bright green and more detailed as Rebane switched the Image Intensifier on. Her chest rose and fell with rapid breaths as she concentrated on his uniform. They wore standard Union camouflage, summer colors. Four men.

How did they find me? Khaled must have told them!

The light from his headlamp scanned the yard and blinded Rebane momentarily.

"Lass mich los—Let me go!" the woman screamed. One of the men grabbed a tuft of her long blonde hair to force her up the stairs. The woman wore nothing but a thin cotton dress and Rebane shivered when she thought of the spanking icy rain. "Ouch!" The woman hit her knee on the top stair.

I should run across the bog, but I'd likely step outside the safe path in the dark. Shit!

Training advised Rebane to stay put and weather the storm. They'd leave eventually, but it didn't take much imagination to guess what would happen to the girl. The last two soldiers remained arguing on the porch. "Lars, it's your graveyard shift."

Rebane smelled tobacco. Their cigarettes glowed in the dark. Someone trashed Rebane's kitchen and the girl screamed again.

"Nein. The place is empty. We don't need a fucking watch."

"You take the first watch, dumb shit. This isn't a negotiation," the second man said, as his cigarette stump hissed in the wet grass. He opened the front door and coarse laughter erupted from the cabin. Rebane smelled the burning birch bark.

So lovely that I made a fire for your drunken asses to stay warm...

Chairs screeched against the floor, followed by breaking glass, thumps and thuds. The woman kept screaming until her voice became a hoarse whisper.

Was I that helpless? Is that what I sounded like when...

Rebane covered her ears because the girl's begging rattled her to the core.

I can't storm in now and fight five armed men.

She felt an urge to go over to her, to take hold of her...

Her entrails knotted, and Rebane's cheeks burned with a high fever. The one called Lars urinated into the bushes—Rebane's most productive raspberry bush—next to her hideout. He removed the cap of a bottle, drained deep gulps and burped. She bet the men inside had found her stepfather's moonshine.

I hope you drink until you're unconscious. I'll make you pay for every drop.

"Verrdamt," the watchman sighed, shifting to a more comfortable position against the flat stone. The face of the moon was on a descent and the long grass blew flat in the icy breeze. The wolves cursed the darkest hour before dawn with a bloodthirsty song, and their voices shook her. Rebane knew to stay away from the radioactive pack that lived in the heart of the forest.

Generations of wolves killing contaminated deer and moose, eating more radiation.

The alpha female began the howling like an air raid siren. The rest of the family echoed with a low wail before the darkness fell silent again. The solid form of the guard tensed. Rebane gaped the lid more as the door creaked. Bare feet slapped on the stone stairs.

Lars, a big man, bolted up with the rifle in his hands. "Stop!"

The skinny blonde leaped down the stairs and darted out on the gravel road. Her hair flipped like a white tail when she ran. Lars shot in the air, the boom echoing from the cliffs and bouncing back from the forest. It worked. The girl halted, raising her hands, her form hunched in defeat.

"I'll shoot you if you don't turn back," Lars yelled.

She turned around and walked toward him, cowering like a runaway dog anticipating the whip. Lars punched her stomach and she folded, doubling in pain. Drenched in sweat, Rebane caught a glimpse of her perplexed, helpless face as the guard banged on the door. The girl looked straight into the darkness where Rebane was with the keen eyes of a Siberian husky. A sprinkle of blood tarnished the rosy shade of her full mouth and Rebane knew she had to save her—at whatever cost.

23.
Liva

The dark velvet of the night had already thinned in the east when Rebane became convinced the Union men had fallen asleep.

A year has passed since we got caught, Daniil and me. Will I come full circle?

She didn't need the NVG. Using the Sig was more comfortable with the naked eye. The guard snored, wrapped into a field blanket for comfort on the hard surface. She placed her feet carefully on the rungs of the ladder and climbed out of the pit. Rebane loomed above him and had to suppress a belch of stomach acid into her sleeve.

She preferred the carotid artery for a fast, silent kill. But the wind whipped at them, making the small hours raw, and Lars lifted his shoulders to protect his neck. He lay on his side with his hands as a pillow. Her knife in an icepick grip, she aimed the double-edged blade at his lower back. Rebane knew what a punch to the kidney did. The interrogators had knocked the wind out of her plenty of times. A stab there meant instant incapacitation.

Her left hand hovered over the sleeping man's mouth while the wood crackled in the branches. A shadow of doubt crossed her face.

I could still run.

Determined, she snuffed his scream. With force and precision, Rebane thrust the stiletto in. She sliced through bundles of nerves and big arteries, releasing a spurt of blood as she removed the spear-point. By the time he'd realized what had taken place, she had rolled him on his back. Rebane opened up his throat while his eyes stared blankly at her. She stood there panting like an asthmatic dog.

I should have avoided the overkill. I snapped the blade against bone.

But upon inspection, the tip of the dagger remained intact. Lars unclenched his fists and slackened. Rebane shoved her hair back. She was drenched in sweat under the raincoat. Muffling her coughs into his blanket before she could continue, she saw her blood on the felt.

I should have stayed in Container City where they have Voodoo priests and medicine witches for the sick.

The sky turned milky-white in an instant and started raining big fluffy snowflakes. The shuffling grass muted Rebane's steps. The birches merged the assassin's shadow amongst their own. She found the window gaped open. A slight wind blew from the east, moving the curtains.

Rebane mounted the crate she'd had placed beneath the window as a safety measure. With a nervous flutter in her stomach, she gazed in between the curtains. A greenish gloom filled the bedroom. Logs crackled in the fireplace, and she smelled the smoke. A fat bastard lay spread across Rebane's bed, clothed from his waist up, but his nether regions were insultingly naked. His rifle leaned against the timber wall in the corner and his mate had curled into Rebane's sleeping bag on the floor.

Climbing back inside proved more difficult than she'd anticipated. Rebane's chest tightened as she lay on her stomach atop the windowsill, but the soldiers never shifted. The man on the bed mumbled something, his eyes rolling behind nervous eyelids. His friend was just as fast asleep. Rebane almost stepped on a puddle of vomit. She flashed a look of distaste.

At least I never puked on the floor. Animals!

She took out her 9mm pistol and caught her breath, undecided.

Which one should I shoot first?

A wet, slurping sound caught her attention, followed by moans from the kitchen. Tiptoeing and pointing the Sig's barrel down, she moved sideways into the corridor. With a stiff stance, Rebane stayed behind the cover of the timber corner. She extended her neck to peek into the twilight kitchen, where the last man held the kneeling woman's head between his hands—the source of the sound was a blow job. The soldier was short, stocky, and had a nose that had been broken at some point. His trousers were at his ankles, but he still wore a fur hat. The man tossed his head back, closing his eyes in enjoyment. The girl's wrists were bound behind her back.

Okay, now I know who to shoot first. Keep sucking, girl.

Rebane took careful aim with both eyes open. Her shoulders relaxed as she breathed evenly. The small red dot from her Aimpoint laser aligned on his forehead, and the cabin became dead silent. *The detour by the Container City proved useful.* A gunsmith had placed the laser atop her Sig with steel mounting after Khaled told him to please Rebane.

The pressure wave from the 9mm couldn't escape the timber structure and caused the windowpanes to jingle. Blood exploded on the logs behind the soldier's head. The woman released his dick as dark liquid rained on her. Rebane let the recoil lift the pistol. A bullet case landed on the floor, issued by the weapon's semi-automatic mechanism. Hot air vibrated above the Aimpoint.

Rebane's ears rang and it took her a few seconds to hear the woman's screams. "Two men in the bedroom! One outside."

Rebane turned to face the bedroom. She knelt sideways and took cover behind the kitchen wall. The center of her sights remained focused on the man who tried to rise from the bedroom floor, unable to untangle his legs from Rebane's sleeping bag. The other one was awake, too, with a stony look on his face. The sleeping bag man's eyes darted toward the rifle in the corner.

"Don't," Rebane hissed.

The Sig spat out a slug. It hit him in the chest, leaving the smell of gunpowder in the room. Bullet fragments tore through his tissues and the internal shock wave ripped into his lungs. Rebane knew she'd hit a major artery because of the blood squirting out of the entry wound. His eyes welled up with tears. It wouldn't take long before hypovolemic shock killed him.

Half-naked number four and Rebane measured each other. He decided to make an asset of his size and bolted up from the bed. The mountain of flesh rammed straight into Rebane while her bullet burrowed useless into the roof trusses.

"Hey!" she screamed when the wind was knocked out of her. It took her a moment to understand the fall had jammed the magazine and the Sig was refusing to work.

Despite his size, the soldier moved with surprising agility. If the girl hadn't intercepted, he would have gotten out of the door. The naked blonde dashed toward him, fell at his feet, and derailed him.

Rebane attacked, stabbing his flesh with quick brutality. The man didn't seem out of breath or even scared. He blocked Rebane with his meaty arms, taking several superficial gashes. Then he hit her with a chair and her blade chinked onto the floor. The girl sank her teeth into his calf but he disposed of her like a goose sheds water. At the same time, Rebane tried to gouge his eyes out.

"Stop, you crazy bitches!" he screamed.

If it weren't for Rebane's next coughing fit, the women could have overpowered him. But she had to bend over doubled in pain and the man got his hands around her throat. When ripping out his hair had no effect, the young girl disengaged. A roaring wind slammed up against the panes.

Rebane tried to loosen the man's fingers but the beast put all of his weight on top her and blocked her windpipe with terrifying finality. She had only seconds before she blacked out. Rebane took hold of his pinkies and twisted them the wrong way. But as soon as she started crawling toward the knife, the soldier mounted Rebane's back, bellowing, "You killed Rudi, you whore. He was like a son to me!"

The giant's knee landed on her neck and pinned Rebane's throat against the floor. The teenager stared at them, puzzled, her complexion glowing and her lips moist. The girl's feet slapped against the hardwood as she ran to the fireplace. Rebane's face turned bright red as she fought for air and the man grunted to press harder. Rebane envisioned how her throat was being crushed.

The youngster's long lily-white fingers held a fire poker. "Hit him," she huffed over her naked shoulder. The teenager's narrow, pretty face looked somber.

Rebane heard the first chirps of birds in the garden. With her last bit of strength, she put her palms on the floor and turned. It rattled the man enough to loosen the death grip and the girl helped by pushing him. Struggling for oxygen,

Rebane got onto her knees, which felt like water. The soldier charged when Rebane got up. She swung the fire poker with all her might and hit his temple.

He hovered like a tall pine about to fall. Rebane bashed his skull until she had to collapse from the pain. The pale girl continued kicking his lifeless head, but Rebane had no strength left. She lay on her side vomiting bile.

Suddenly, the girl looked down at her with tears in her big blue eyes. Rebane realized she must look savage covered in the men's blood. A moth danced around the storm lantern. With each minute, the room grew lighter. The girl's hair was feathery-fine, almost platinum, which fit the porcelain tone of her skin.

Rebane leaned against her elbows amidst a sticky, disgusting pool of blood. The dead man's eyes remained open. She turned her attention to the teenager's protruding belly. "You're pregnant," she said.

At least five months along if I know anything.

She responded with slow nod. "Yes, that's why they took me," the girl replied in her self-contained way. "Would you mind cutting the rope? I can't feel my fingers."

"Of course."

The girl sat on Papa's chair rubbing her wrists. Rebane placed her ruined raincoat on her narrow shoulders and promised, "I'll get you some clean clothes."

You can't be older than sixteen.

"I'm Liva." The youngster's eyes were fierce and passionate now. "Löwe is my last name. I'm seventeen—that's what you were wondering, right?"

What do you know—a mind reader.

"It means lion," Rebane replied. "Your last name."

A German girl in my cabin. I'm neck-deep in shit.

Along with her next cough, she tasted blood.

"And you're seriously ill, if I know anything." Liva stated the obvious. "Sit down and I'll have a look." Her hand felt cool against Rebane's burning forehead. "You have a high fever. It could be over thirty-nine degrees Celsius. Such a temperature can damage brain tissue." Liva used the hem of the raincoat to wipe the men's blood off Rebane's throat. Her sleek index finger paused over Rebane's carotid artery. Rebane felt the jolt of energy that flowed from Liva's touch.

The young woman's fair brows scrunched. "Your pulse is too fast. That's Zombie Dust— what you're sick with. You're not a local?" As Liva the Lion spoke, a rosy shade flooded her cheekbones. In the light of the cold, raw day, Rebane saw the dawning bruise below her left eye. Whoever had hit her was righthanded.

"I am, but I've been…um…traveling for the last ten years," Rebane blurted.

A stupid lie.

Rebane knew she couldn't fool the gaze of those blazing eyes for a second.

Liva offered a thoughtful, sad smile. "Everyone here has immunity. Some say the disease was a biological weapon that escaped from a lab, but I think it's a punishment from the Goddess."

"The Goddess?"

"Mielikki, the Queen of the Forest."

"Yes, I've heard of her. I hope you're worthy of your name because now we have to hack these raping lunatics into pieces."

"Why don't we dig a hole in the ground?" Liva asked. She stepped over the dead body to put a kettle on the stove. She opened the cupboards in search of matches.

What a wise ass.

"You're welcome to dig five graves. The ground is already frozen solid below the top layer. The work takes several days, and they may have friends—armed friends. Get dressed. You have to help me. I'm not as strong as I used to be."

24.
Contaminated Wolves

"Why don't you just leave their clothes on?" Liva asked, trying to breathe through her mouth.

The air was bracing, but not cold enough to ward off the stink of death. Pertti's oversized overalls hung on the girl's petite frame. Liva settled the bandana over her nose and mouth. The ground lay covered with a thin film of snow.

"I don't want them recognized if someone comes looking," Rebane explained with her mouth set hard. She tried to rip the shirt off Lars' back, but the corpse had stiffened and wouldn't agree to turn. She straightened her back with a grimace of pain. "The wolves can leave shreds behind." A few flies resurrected from wherever they spent their winters and Rebane banished them with a wave of her hand. The fastest females had already laid eggs on the Union men's exposed flesh.

"You'll feed them to the wolves?" Liva asked with a timid look. "Not that I care what happens to the bodies, but aren't the animals dangerous to us?"

Rebane glanced at her accomplice with a knowing smile. "Not if we get the meat there before dark. This pack has tasted humans before. They'll recognize the delicacy on tonight's menu. Now hold his leg up so I can cut the tendons. My back hurts and I don't want to vomit from the pain. I must keep down some food."

Liva pressed her rosy lips together with a determined expression on her face. She grabbed the man by the ankle with both hands. His backside had turned black and his stomach had swelled with gas. Rebane opened Lars's skin around his hip joint and serrated the crisscrossing ligaments which connected his thigh to his pelvis. When his legs came loose, she devoted her attention to dismembering his arms.

Rebane checked on the younger woman from time to time, but Liva studied the procedure with calm interest. Rebane placed the tip of the butcher's knife between the bony cup and the upper end of the humerus bone. She cut the tendons and muscles with expert precision. The soldier's arm loosened from the torso. Next, Rebane dug for the atlas vertebrae in his neck. She swore at the effort it took her to sever his head while Liva admired the cold, cloudy day.

"You're the wanted woman the men talked about?" There was a note of finality in Liva's voice.

The twitch in Rebane's cheek revealed that she was clenching her teeth. "No," she denied, irritated. Her hard work had saturated the grass with dark, clogged blood. She sharpened her knives for the third time because the blades dulled against the men's bones. Rebane knotted the sleeves of the mechanic's overalls around her narrow waist and went to work on the second body. Liva tailed her and lifted, pulled, and twisted as Rebane ordered.

The end of August sun radiated soothing warmth when Rebane cut the last bone loose in the late afternoon. She sat on the flat stone, exhausted. "Just give me a minute." Liva sat next to her, nodding in agreement. Rebane closed her eyes to bathe in the light, but the inquisitive stare of the younger woman bothered her. The overgrown grass expelled whispers as the wind moved in the garden.

"You're going to take me there in the end anyway," Liva stated.

"What the fuck are you talking about?" Rebane stared at the girl with a stab of anxiety in her chest. Liva held her head high, her ivory shoulders pushed back.

"To the Union airbase. My tea leaves said so," Liva whispered. A shadow of a cloud passed across her face. "Mielikki appeared in my dream. She told me my child would die if I didn't get to a doctor in time."

"Tea leaves? The Forest Queen? Did you remember to check your crystal ball? No, you'll be fine. You're young and strong." As Rebane met her gaze, she understood that the girl believed in what she said. Rebane had no desire to rattle her. "Look, dreams conjure our worst fears." Rebane's limbs hurt and she felt an irresistible need to lay down in the sun to rest. "I just saved your life. And now you want me to enter the wolf's lair and be killed."

"No, I saved you. That big bastard would have strangled you if I didn't bring you the fire poker."

"You can think so if you like that version better," Rebane said with a chuckle. Rusty blood had dried under her fingernails because it had seeped through the leather gloves.

Liva's lips narrowed into a line before she spoke again. "Rebane, you must run or attack—there is no in between. This isn't a safe place, not even during the winter."

Rebane placed her hand over Liva's and enjoyed the cool silk of the girl's skin. "I know, Meine Freundin. I'll run farther north right after you heal me with your divine powers. Tell Mielikki to pay better attention to my prayers."

Liva gave her a serious look. "Now you're mocking me. That's unfair. I come from a long lineage of seers and healers," she said, pouting. "My dad was a doctor."

"Why did the Union men drag you along, anyway? If they were on a mission, you slowed them down." Rebane slowly shook her head as she rose to button up Dad's overalls. After the short rest, she shivered. Her fever had returned. She gazed at the straight, dusty road and made a mental note to repair the alarm wires.

"Because they are..." Liva paused to look at the severed hands in a pile of body parts, "they were men. They saw a young woman running from the Container gang's northern outpost after they blew the place sky high. They wanted to fuck me or sell me—or both." Liva placed her hands, which ended in perfect oval nails, on her stomach. "But my baby is okay. She kicks, you know."

Rebane felt a sting of compassion. "I'm sorry you had to go through all that." Her eyes narrowed because the sun gazed at them from the clouds.

Liva's large, light-blue eyes stared into hers. "Don't think you should have come for me earlier. I was a slave in the glacier outpost. I'm used to—well, you know what I mean."

Better than you'll ever know.

Insects buzzed lazily above the meat, but dark clouds assembled above the forest. "Help me get the wheelbarrow, witchy woman," Rebane said and walked across the yard behind the house. When she glanced over her shoulder, she saw how the long garden angelicas divided before Liva. The grass waved like seaweed around the girl.

Magic, after all. Perhaps I need Mielikki's priestess on my side.

Rebane forced the squeaky wheel, which needed filling, across the turf. Liva, sweating in Rebane's flannel shirt under Pertti's overalls, pulled from the front.

The birds had stopped singing and the sun shone low, already touching the jagged outline of the forest. They grunted and panted while they packed the first load, covering the mangled body parts with a tarpaulin. They did well on the leveled ground, but their vehicle jammed into the first ditch. Rebane's boots took in muddy water from the bottom, but she decided to swallow her curse. From the river came the cawing of the last seagulls.

"Wait here," Rebane said and launched off running toward the house. She returned with wooden planks, which she placed atop the ditch. Emerging from the direction of the swamp, a spotted owl spread its wings. The nocturnal bird soared high above the blood-red of an impending sunset. Heart thumping in her chest, Rebane knew that the sounds of life from the marshland would silence within weeks, and the wolves would roam closer to her cabin. She spied Liva from the corner of her eye and hoped that the girl would stay.

I don't want to be alone in the darkness. After she gives birth there will be three of us.

If the German girl had suffered at the hands of the dead men, nothing had reached the surface, only the black eye. Liva offered an encouraging smile. "Soldier on, warrior woman. We can't give up now." A sparkle of courage flashed in her eyes—the most incredible eyes, similar to those Rebane had seen on arctic sled dogs. The women settled for a meadow which punctured the heart of the forest with an opening. They dumped their first load on the moist ground and headed back to the house for a refill.

The thawed snow had frozen under the trees, and the second wheelbarrow load moved easier when they followed the snowline. As they trekked back to the house for the third time, the stillness had become almost unnatural.

"This place gives me goosebumps," Liva whispered as they reached the meadow again. She almost lost her balance as she stumbled on a skull that lay stark white against the moss. "If I can smell the rot, won't the canines pick it up?" Rebane didn't reply but concentrated on rubbing her shoulder muscles, which ached from the close combat of last night. The northern wind hurled icy flakes at them, and the air became denser and more bracing. Liva had borrowed Rebane's wool beanie and her white braids flapped against her back as she picked up speed and pushed the empty wheelbarrow. She crossed the ditch along the planks with precision and Rebane struggled to keep up with her.

"Yes, you're right. The wolves smell blood from miles away if the wind blows right," Rebane said as they reached the safety of her home. The women stood under the birches lining the road to her cabin. "They're usually timid, intelligent animals, but these ones are different, completely crazy because of the radiation that contaminated their diet for decades. We can only hope they prefer the buffet table over chasing us."

When they finished loading the last body onto the wheelbarrow—the man who fought the hardest—Rebane had drained all of her strength. Her windpipe hurt. She had difficulty breathing past the spot where the giant had strangled her.

"Liva, wait," Rebane huffed. "Give me a second." She leaned her back against a spotted birch trunk and spat blood on the frosted ground.

Liva's eyes were wide with suspense. They appeared almost white in the twilight haze. "Reb, I know you hurt, but we must continue. We can't stay here. The smell will lead the wolves to your yard, and we won't be able to step out the door." When the skinny girl embraced Rebane, some of her strength seemed to transfer between their bodies.

"Reb, now!" Liva urged, taking the handgrips of the wheelbarrow. Rebane pulled from the front braces.

The eye of the bog had swallowed the sun and the fog gathered its forces among the trees. Rebane thought she felt the eyes of the predators on her skin when they bordered the forest meadow for the final time. The dry leaves shuffled in the wind. A breeze evaporated the sweat from her scalp and a shiver crept between her aching shoulder blades. Rebane, a trained killer, couldn't keep the radioactive wolves out of her head. She feared to stare long into the night that stalked them from the conifer forest. The aggressive alfa female commanded a well-rehearsed team that blocked the escape route of their prey. She'd once witnessed a bull moose stand chest-deep in an icy river for seven hours to ward off these wolves.

Things hadn't ended well for him. The Queen liked to eat her victims alive and kicking.

Liva and Rebane struggled to roll the last torso onto the pile. Rebane straightened herself and remembered she'd left her night-vision goggles at home.

A mistake that could cost our lives.

The middle of the meadow where the duo stood was bathed in dim green. She looked sideways at the forest rim and let her eyes adapt to the dark.

Liva's hand searched for Rebane's. Her fingers squeezed hard. "There, between the trees," she said, her voice barely audible.

Rebane sensed Liva's fear, and she withdrew the Sig from her belt holster. The wolf stood between the young alders gazing at them with a pair of yellow eyes. The lush branches covered the animal's body but Rebane could see the outlines of a fluffy Siberian husky-like mask. Rebane's legs shook like jelly.

"Liva, don't move. Be silent," she whispered, her voice full of tension. She followed the female with her barrel, but the darkness sided with the wolves.

I don't know how many wolves the alpha pair has raised.

The enormous size of the animal became evident when the she-wolf trod toward them without a sound. Rebane led Liva by the hand—away from the carcasses.

Rebane felt something soft brush against her arm. An enormous male passed her without even looking at her. The outlines of the third predator detached from the dark behind Liva's back, the wolf's neck hair raised spiky against the milky mist. The low growl wasn't more than a whispered warning. More shadows gathered from different directions after the Queen reached the corpses. She exposed her fangs. The saliva-dripping grimace transformed the beautiful canine face into a mask of the Devil. The alpha female's ears pressed flat against her head and her eyes glowed with hot sulfur. The animal's back arched as she robbed a foot and sent a man's head rolling across the ground.

The women retreated, keeping their eyes on the wolves who snapped at each other while their jaws crunched bone. Liva and Rebane left the wheelbarrow behind and sprinted toward the house. They didn't stop running until they reached the garden.

It rained hail as Liva gathered the deserters' clothes into a pile by the light of Rebane's headlamp. She covered the evidence with dirt and leaves, placing stones on top. Rebane stood on the porch with the loaded rifle in her hands. Twigs crackled. She pointed the barrel of the Tikka at the noise but breathed a sigh of relief when a large buck raised an antler-crowned head from the grass. From afar, the savage choir of canine voices echoed behind the forest. The deer escaped into the willows in two enormous leaps.

"Who is that?" Liva whispered next to Rebane's ear.

"Just a buck."

"No, there!" Liva pointed to the field where the rye shot out tender stalks.

Listening avidly, Rebane saw the shadow of a man just before he jumped over the ditch and merged into the darkness at the back of the yard.

25.
Healer

Rebane leaned against the dry bark of the alder. The red fox stopped to sniff at the ground some sixty-five feet ahead of her, then trotted onward. The white point of his tail vanished among the foliage. Rebane knew the route with her eyes shut but wondered why she wore only a T-shirt and panties. The forest path ended where the drifting mists swallowed the flame-colored animal. She felt compelled to catch the creature, which reappeared on top of a fallen tree. He sat on the soft moss with his pointed ears moving on top of his head—listening, like a fine-tuned antenna. It took her a moment to understand that her shirt was wet with something that had the sharpest evil smell.

"Loki, get out," Liva's voice commanded. She sat on a chair next to Rebane's bed. But Loki, the fox, wore an offended face. He hopped on the floor and bent double to scratch his neck with a soot-colored paw.

"How are you feeling, dear friend?" Liva asked Rebane.

"Better, I guess..." Rebane propped herself up against her elbows. "Hey, you—you peed on me!" Rebane yelled at the fox, who gazed at her with his slit irises.

"It's a sure sign that he likes you, marking his turf," Liva said and wiped Rebane's hair off her face. "The fever is gone. You'll live."

"How did you manage to catch a fox?" Rebane asked, still baffled. "They escape the best hunters because they can smell a human miles away." She placed her feet on the cold floor and Liva steadied her as she stood.

Rebane rummaged through the closet and grabbed a clean tank top and a pair of men's trousers, which she secured with a leather belt. She pushed her head through the neckline of the woolly sweater and looked out the window. The yellow irises and plantains that grew by the riverbed had withered. Snow covered the grass and robbed the yard of color. The fog from her dream hovered over the field of stubble. The porch floor creaked and yanked Rebane out of her thoughts. Her hand searched for the gun belt that wasn't there.

"Relax, it's only him," Liva assured, peeking into the kitchen. "Bjorn. "
Why did you let that snake inside?

"Sit down, both of you," Liva ordered and drew a chair for Rebane. The air in the kitchen soon turned blue with the smoke from Bjorn's cigarettes. He chain-smoked like a chimney.

"Liva is a shaman," Bjorn started as he removed his hobnailed boots. "I've never met anyone who can travel to Tuonela—the land of the dead—and come back unharmed."

You're joking, right?

"The ferrywoman remembers your name. She's let me cross twice," Liva explained, checking to see if Rebane believed her or not. "The spell I fetched for you cost me three years of my life."

"How can you know I've met the ferrywoman?" Rebane asked before she could hold her tongue. The puddle of blood was gone. She remembered that bits of brain tissue had stuck between the floorboards, but now the cabin looked clean and polished. Logs crackled in the fireplace. "Bjorn helped me clean up the mess," Liva explained and sharpened a knife. "After you almost shot him."

"I don't remember any of that," Rebane whispered.

Liva found the tinderbox, and another kettle of water soon boiled happily on the stove.

"When you fell on the porch unconscious, your rifle went off. The .308 is still inside one of the birches. That tree saved my life." Bjorn laughed and smoothed his beard.

Then the fox cried out with its strange language that always sounded as if the animal is in distress. Liva rose to open the door, and Loki dashed out as if he'd always been the young woman's pet and knew the house rules.

"Liva couldn't leave you alone for a minute," Bjorn added." You almost died, Reb."

"Stop calling me that." Rebane bit her lip and tasted blood.

Bjorn shifted his weight. "Everyone else gets the Zombie Dust as a child. The virus kills half of the people who contract it as adults."

Rebane took a piece of dark bread and wondered if it would stay down. She felt lightheaded. "How did you catch the fox?" she asked Liva again.

"I didn't catch him. I asked your spirit animal to come because you needed help," the girl said. "He padded straight into the bedroom and curled on your tummy." Liva paused to set the dented plates on the table. "The witchcraft demands that the shaman addresses a *Vulpes vulpes* by his secret name—his mom named this fellow Loki because he is a trickster." Liva's eyes narrowed and she offered Rebane an enigmatic smile as she sipped her nettle tea.

Rebane didn't want to sound ungrateful and didn't press the matter further. "You must eat to get your strength back," Liva said and placed a slice of smoked meat on Rebane's plate.

"Loki also peed everywhere and made dreadful noises all night," Bjorn explained. "But I don't mind so much if you feel better." He spoke with his mouth full. "My aunt died of Zombie Dust."

"And why did you invade my home in the first place?" Rebane's voice dripped with all the venom she had left. She leaned back in her chair because her legs felt like jelly.

"I gathered ginger, black pepper and cloves for you," Bjorn continued with his quiet humor and brushed water droplets from his hair. "There's snow everywhere. It wasn't easy. But Liva can do wonders with poor ingredients."

Liva unwrapped another tin foil and revealed a chunk of salted moose. Rebane couldn't taste anything but swallowed another bite. She spied Liva from the corner of her eye.

Dreams about foxes mean not to trust someone. It's a warning about a false friend—and these two seem too friendly with each other.

"I promised Khaled I would contact you," Bjorn explained further. The chair wailed under him. Rebane caught a glimpse of the Smith and Wesson on his belt next to a long Lapland knife.

Her rifle stood neatly in the gun rack ten feet away. Liva rose to let Loki in after the fox scratched the front door in a frenzy. He sat under the table with his fluffy, warm side pressed against Rebane's shin. Liva lit the oil lamp on the counter. A hint of sulfur lingered from the tinderbox while Rebane and Bjorn measured each other. His mouth remained a thin line.

"Go on," Rebane suggested.

The fire crackled and popped as Bjorn spoke. "Captain Karasholi sent me to check on the Union commander because you wanted to know. The man is tall and has sand-colored hair—a colonel. The career military type. He looks as if he swallowed a stake. Reb, you know what I mean."

"Uh-hum," she managed to utter under the surge of dark memories.

They made the monster a colonel after he let a GRU spy slip through his net?

She clung to the last shred of hope.

Maybe it's not him.

"The man terrifies the shit out of my liaison officer," Bjorn added between slurps of hot tea.

I know what you mean.

If there was a moon in the sky, the clouds had snuffed it out with darkness. Rebane's reflection on the window looked like her old self. The olive color had returned to her skin and her eyes reflected her determination. "And the name?"

"His name is Aldrich Weisser. Khaled said that you share a history with this man."

"Yes, you could put it that way."

Liva wore Rebane's brown hunting trousers with the top button open. The flannel shirt struggled to stretch over her enormous belly.

How far along are you, my friend? You can't run with me, and I can't leave you with Bjorn.

"It wasn't easy to get through the siege ring," he added and swallowed a mouthful.

"I'll bet Weisser opened it for you." Rebane stared daggers at him.

"No! I endangered my life to warn you..." Bjorn cut her short with genuine anger in his voice. He turned to the teenager. "I already told Liva what happened."

Liva stopped braiding her hair. "Yes, my runes say he tells the truth." She dug something out of her pocket—light grey stones with strange markings carved on them.

Rebane saw the hesitant hope in Bjorn's blue eyes. "Khaled asked for you. They need every trained soldier. I promised to return with you. The Union besieges Container City. They won't get food or water before they surrender unconditionally."

Bjorn gazed at Liva. "You should come too. You'd be better off with us." Bjorn's eyes darted between the women.

You're afraid.

Liva laced her hands together on top of her belly. It astonished Rebane how perfect her profile was. The cutest cupid's bow crowned Liva's mouth.

Rebane rubbed her hands down her thighs.

I can't leave you and your baby to die. You saved my life.

With a knot tightening in her entrails, she fetched the gun belt from the rack and checked the Sig's magazine. When conversation ceased, the silence grew thicker by the minute. Bjorn and Liva waited for her reply. Rebane's worst enemy had gathered his forces forty miles south, but the certainty of battle felt easier than the shapeless fear which had plagued her for a year.

Liva looked at Rebane with fascinated awe.

Perhaps I sealed my fate that night...when I couldn't leave you at the mercy of the Union men.

26.
Air Raid

Rebane could no longer feel her toes. Chills rushed through her because the sweat from dragging the sled dried fast. She turned around halfway up the ridge and noticed Liva struggling to follow. Here, old pines and spruces had weathered the nuclear war. With each step, Rebane fought wind-driven heaps of snow that gathered between the trunks. The first clouds of dawn formed in the sky.

"Wait! I can't climb that fast," Liva called. She sat in the snow, bent like a folding knife. "I told you this would happen," she blubbered, her face rigid with fear.

"What would happen?" Rebane asked, out of breath from running downhill, but the younger woman didn't answer. Liva lay on her side in the soft snow. Rebane took the radio from her breast pocket. "Alpha One. We're slow. Over and out." She waited for Bjorn's reply but received only white noise. "Maybe he's out of range. The hilltop must block the signal." The breeze ravaged the women, as cold as a knife.

"Augh!" Liva wailed. Her stomach had descended, now a bulge against her pelvis. She had opened the buttons of her fur coat. "I can't split now. There's a month to go," she cried out.

"You won't," Rebane assured, kneeling, she put her arm around the girl's shoulders. "It's just a spasm. It will pass. When we get to the Container City, we'll find a midwife for you."

"This will take a lot more than a midwife. I need an ultrasound," she added, her face whiter than the snow-covered ground, "and an operating theater."

"You mean that's what the tealeaves said?"

Liva nodded. In the valley below, the morning broke with honey-colored clouds. The forest grew lighter.

Rebane struggled to find the right words. "I asked Bjorn, and he can't take you to the Union airbase. He abandoned his mission to come to my cabin. And who says that you'll be safe there? What if they just let you die?"

"And you know I don't mean Bjorn. I asked *you*—the only person I trust with my baby girl's life." Liva's quicksilver energy returned with the rosy pink that settled on her cheekbones. The pain eased.

"I can't step into the base!" Rebane snapped. "They'll torture me. Only the

Forest Goddess knows how long I'd pray for death before he'd put a bullet into the back of my skull."

"If you don't take me there, my child will die and drag me to the underworld with her." Liva met Rebane's stare with fearless eyes. "You're smart. You'll outwit him—just as you did before."

The sun climbed out of the forest. Rebane tried to collect herself before she spoke. "I didn't outwit Weisser. A fly never beats the spider. He let me go after he had his fun." Rebane shifted her weight from one foot to the other. "Has your pain passed?" she asked, petting Liva's long straight hair which she wore parted in the middle.

"Yes."

"You see? It's normal." Rebane pulled her cap down over her ears and fumbled in her pockets for a second set of gloves. She spied the younger woman with anxious eyes.

When you set your mind on something, you never take no for an answer.

"What do you know about giving birth?" Liva asked in a-matter-of-fact voice. "Take off your gloves and feel my tummy." She grunted as she searched for a comfortable position, pushing the lowest branches away from her face. Rebane didn't know what to search for. "Press harder," Liva urged and directed Rebane's fingers. "Otherwise, you won't feel it. The child folds her feet against her buttocks. She turned and comes out feet first. The baby will get stuck into my pelvis."

"Reb?" the radio buzzed. "I'm coming around the hill," Bjorn's voice said through the crackle. He reached the women with his rifle slung over his shoulder. He wore a worried expression which he tried to hide as he saw the trouble with Liva. Bjorn was big and stocky, and most of the time nothing could rattle his confidence. A cigarette dangled out of his mouth.

Rebane cast a disapproving glare. "I wish you wouldn't smoke near the baby."

"Sorry," he apologized. Spots of red appeared on his cheeks. He drew a final breath of smoke and stumped the cigarette into the snow. "The helicopter never came." He looked away as he spoke. "I fired both flares Khaled gave you." He handed the binoculars to Rebane.

"Something is wrong with the city. It's too quiet around here," Rebane said. "And Liva claims her fetus is upside down. You wouldn't happen to have an idea of how to turn it?"

"We still had a hospital with a maternity ward when my sister Maria gave birth to her son. I'm sure the midwife of Red Lotus knows how to execute a controlled tilt."

"That's what I've been telling her all morning," Rebane huffed. Their eyes met. Rebane tugged her pants up.

You smell the smoke as well. Something burns.

"Reb, you carry the ammo crate so Liva can sit in the sled," Bjorn suggested. "I'll pull her. We shouldn't exercise the mother."

Rebane's legs shook from the exertion of climbing this far. Her back ached under the combined weight of the rucksack and rifle. A scattering of snow fell, and the sky clouded over a dull gray. She decided not to bitch, but her eyes narrowed into slits.

Four or five miles of rugged terrain. I wish I'd regained my strength.

"How far are we from the Container City?" Bjorn asked when the valley dawned behind the shoulder of the next forest-covered ridge. His face was flushed red and he leaned his hands on his knees.

"I'm fine. I have a perfect set of legs," Liva suggested. "I can walk."

A spark landed on Rebane's windbreaker. She smothered it out with her hand. Liva rose and Rebane settled the ammo crate on the sled. Liva's chest rose and fell with rapid breaths. She tried to hide a grimace.

With an icy dread, Rebane lay on top of the ridge. She wiped her scarf over the lenses of the binoculars. "Less than a mile," she replied to Bjorn in an even, clipped voice, "but I don't think anyone from the City can help us." The leaves felt damp. The snow melted from her body heat.

A wall of smoke drifted into view, riding the winds from the south. "Get down!" she yelled. But Bjorn and Liva had already found cover among the pines. The rotational hum grew deafening before the aircraft rose above the tree line. The Boeing AH-64D Apache Longbow followed the curvature of the terrain, whipping up turbulent snow as it dived into the cove. The treetops bowed like a rye field in the wind, and Rebane held onto her beanie. It was an attack helicopter painted matte green and armed with air-to-ground weaponry—rockets and grenade launchers—the works. Explosions shook the hillside and the trees shed their snow cover onto the people huddled below. Silence vibrated in the air before the next rocket hit its mark.

Bjorn's face turned ashen. His knuckles whitened when he grabbed his rifle—useless against the military helicopters buzzing over the ruins of Container City like a swarm of flies. He wrapped a meaty arm around Liva's shoulders. There was a look of pain in Liva's pale eyes.

The blood-red of the burning Citadel, the mushroom cloud of smoke, filled the air with deadly fumes. The next grenades wreaked havoc on a group of refugees, families who'd attempted to run into the forest. A row of rockets embellished the Apache's wings as it banked hard left. The last standing watchtower returned the fire with machine guns, trying to hit the enemy pilots. Rebane's stomach clenched.

The last stronghold of resistance has fallen. Nothing can stop the Union forces now.

The sky turned red from the fire, which smoldered and crackled as it engulfed the custom-made trailers, the people, and their livestock. Glass exploded and toxic fumes rose as gasoline and plastic burned. Rebane's eyes flashed at Bjorn and then at Liva. She flattened into the snowdrift when the formation of helicopters climbed the cliffside, exiting their target zone.

Khaled...

Then the attack fleet was gone, and the site became dead silent. Rebane adjusted the zoom rings of her binoculars, trying to find Khaled's team. Black smoke drifted at the ceiling level of the outermost containers, slid under the doorframes of passageways, and smothered anyone still alive inside. What remained of Mad Dog's soldiers, riding crawlers, sped past the running civilians. Rebane balled her fist. None of the faces rang a chord in her heart.

She drew a sharp breath when she understood that Liva would get no help from a midwife there. The pregnant woman lay on the ground under a fir tree which had shed its needles on the frozen snow. Bjorn shielded her with his large, fleshy body. His chubby face was red with cold or emotion and his breath misted above their heads. Rebane could see the hesitant hope die in Liva's glassy eyes as she looked at her with knowing. The teenager's face had paled whiter than usual. Bjorn awaited orders, but Rebane faced the other way to hide her inner turmoil.

I can't take you to the base. We must run north, and I need Bjorn's assistance.

Rebane turned her attention to the valley where a flock of livestock had escaped from their herders. When the sheepdogs barked at them, snapping at the sheep's ankles in an attempt for control, the panicked animals made a U-turn. Every sheep followed the ram into the flames and their cries filled the air. Rebane covered her mouth with her hand.

She collected herself and jumped to her feet when Liva cried out. She removed the fur hood and saw that Liva's hair was glued onto her face with sweat. Bjorn turned away.

You knew.

Liva arched her back against the tree and screamed.

"Liva, how long have you been in labor?" Rebane asked, irritated.

"Light contractions started after midnight ten hours ago," she said between her panting. "They are stronger and more frequent now. And they last longer."

"Why didn't you tell me?" There was hurt in Rebane's voice as she towered above Liva and Bjorn with her arms akimbo. "Have you tried pushing yet?"

"Rebane, of course not!" Liva shouted before she grimaced to endure the next wave of agony. "No, no... I can't give birth in the middle of a battle," she mumbled through the tears that ran down her cheeks.

Rebane felt the ravages of the wind again. It worried her that the next night might bring minus four degrees Fahrenheit or colder.

You could die of hypothermia if you bleed. I don't know what to do.

"Bjorn, go see if the soldiers can help us," Rebane commanded. "Locate Khaled if you can." She tried to look determined, but her voice broke at the end of her sentence.

"No need for that," a man replied. Snow fell from the sky with large flakes, turning the scenery white. Rebane squinted to see past the rain.

Khaled's eyes wore grim darkness as he climbed the cliff and waded through the snow. Two of his Russian lieutenants followed, carrying a machine gun.

27.
Birth

Khaled zipped up his camo jacket and lifted his snow goggles. "I can spare one ATV and that's it. No men..." Rebane felt uncomfortable under the straightforwardness of his stare.

"Not even Bjorn?" she asked. Desperation strangled Rebane's throat, but she met his eyes with a fixed expression on her face.

"No. You're on your own," Captain Karasholi said. He turned to Bjorn. "Lieutenant Rask, we need to defend the refugees. Ya'laa managed to run and shall regroup her people."

Rebane kneeled to look below the all-terrain vehicle. "There may not be enough clearance. The rear axle is packed with sleet." Bjorn helped her clear the brakes and the shock absorbers.

"There will be a storm tonight. Lots of powdered snow," the Finnish man commented. He moved like someone wading through water. "You must leave now. It's not safe around us." He gazed at Liva, worried.

Rebane battled to join the toboggan's binds to the towing hook of the arctic cat. She forced the straps into a knot, tightening the buckles to make sure. Khaled delivered a set of commands to the Russians and shifted his weight, impatient because of the waiting. The man had a slab of a face, hard to read.

This is the last time I will see you.

Rebane felt a sinking in her stomach as she spied Khaled from the corner of her eye.

"Help me tie Liva to the toboggan," she urged Bjorn.

Liva's fists clenched as they helped her stand. "I'll be okay," she said, breathing fast. "You don't need to strap me down."

But Bjorn didn't take no for an answer. "If you lose consciousness because of the pain and Reb drives fast…it's a bumpy ride across the ice field." He secured Liva onto the sled with loops of wide leather belts that ran under her armpits. Her stomach looked as if it would explode any minute, and Rebane feared she would bleed out on the way there.

Khaled appeared a ball of tension and his voice grew hoarse. "The ATV may run out of gas, but I'll give you a set of skis and a pulling harness just to make sure. You have a compass, Reb?" Rebane forced herself to smile at him.

"Yes, and my beef jerky. It's only ten miles. We'll manage." She gave a fractured laugh. Her hair flapped around her face in the breeze before she gathered it under her beanie. "Goodbye," Rebane whispered.

Khaled stared at her with his brown-green eyes. She could see he was hesitating, but Rebane put her arms around him, and he returned the desperate squeeze. "Stay alive," he whispered into her ear, "and come back to us."

Rebane swallowed the lump in her throat. Bjorn followed the others into the gorge where the surviving trucks lifted clouds of snow. *Thank you*, Rebane formed with her lips—the shade of blueberries from the cold, but Bjorn didn't turn to look at the women again. Rebane mounted the ATV and turned the ignition key, and the motor rumbled into life. The fuel meter flickered at half full and then settled on a quarter as Khaled had warned.

I have no idea how much the engine uses in rugged terrain.

She followed the shoreline which glittered in daylight. The wind swooshed in her ears, and she could no longer feel the pinch of frostbite on her nose. The pebbles scratched the bottom of the toboggan and Liva held onto the wooden beams. The toboggan molded and inclined with the dunes. Liva knew to lean to the opposite side as Rebane followed a curve around some cliffs. Soon the cloud wall became thicker and shrouded the scenery.

Her breath fogged in the beam of her headlamp when she stopped to check on Liva and their heading. Rebane estimated that they had little over three miles to go, and with some imagination, she could picture the airfield behind the blizzard. The ATV made its way between the sleek dunes. The landscape could have been the surface of the moon. Windburn stole all sensations from Rebane's cheeks and earlobes.

The ozone smell of fresh snow greeted her, and the tailwind lifted a cloud of snow behind them.

Liva's eyes blinked almost white when Rebane stopped to look at her in the light of the headlamp. The smell of vomit revealed that she had puked on the fur coat. "I can't breathe! The air is too cold," Liva complained. Her cheeks were red from windblown snow. Liva's forehead burned, although the freezing gales did everything in their power to rip the women apart.

You have a fever.

"Keep the scarf in front of your mouth," Rebane replied. "Does the pain pass for a moment?"

"No, it's constant now. What a stupid question!" Liva yelled. Then she asked, still with angry eyes, "Do you carry moonshine?"

"I wouldn't give you alcohol even if I had a distillery on board," Rebane replied, offended. "It's just a contraction. Remember how far you've already come. I can see the airbase lights," she lied. Wood crackled in the trunks of the birches which defied the emptiness of the landscape by taking root here.

Liva's hands knotted on the fabric of Rebane's windbreaker. "I'll die without pain relief!" she yelled and pulled Rebane closer with horrible strength. "There's a ring of fire between my legs." When Liva's swollen body finally relaxed, she gasped, "I can't take it anymore. I must push."

Whatever you do, don't push," Rebane shouted and mounted her ride. "You'll put pressure on the umbilical cord, and you'll crush the baby."

As if I know what may happen if she pushes.

She looked back at Liva when she turned the throttle handle. The ATV pulled the toboggan clear from the field where spear-like ice puckered from the ground.

Beyond a stretch of the whiteness, the landing lights of the base airfield mirrored an orange hue on the low-hanging clouds. The afternoon took a darker turn because no light penetrated the clouds. The snow, which was lightness itself while spinning in the air, resisted the vehicle when it layered dunes on the ground. The ATV coughed and its headlamps died a second before the power went off.

"Fuck! Not now," Rebane cursed and turned the ignition switch twice. The arctic cat went through a series of shakes and coughs, but she forced the engine to run on fuel vapor.

When the watchtower's searchlight blinded Rebane, she blinked to get rid of the black spots in her vision. She slowed down before they would shoot them.

Try to stay cold and clear. You survived him before.

She didn't fear death, but she dreaded Weisser with the atavistic fear of a snared rabbit. She couldn't beat him—not on his soil.

"Halt!" the order from the tower rang. The arctic cat obeyed by turning off the power. Rebane glanced over her shoulder at Liva, who huddled unconscious aboard the sled.

Rebane lifted her hands as a signal of capitulation. The soldiers surrounded them with their assault rifles cocked. Rebane pleaded for Liva. "The woman is German. Of your people. She must get to the operation table immediately. Please see that she gets to the doctor."

The men stared baffled at Liva's belly, then at Rebane, who added, "The child is stuck in the birth canal. Help her!" Rebane grabbed the captain by his sleeve and met the steel in his eyes. "Promise me."

He nodded and barked to the soldiers, "Help the woman."

"Name? Age? Military rank?" the captain rapped questions at Rebane with a clipped voice. He was a tall, wiry man in his forties with a downturned mouth and a stony face. He wore a long black overcoat like all the Union officers during wintertime. The visor of his cap shaded his eyes now, but Rebane sensed his excitement.

She answered the questions truthfully. "Yes. I'm wanted for murder," she admitted. "But I don't care. Just help her." Her voice faltered near the end.

One of the soldiers wrenched her hands behind her back for cuffing. Rebane expected to feel a flood of relief by now.

My fate is confirmed, I'll be at peace. No more running.

But her terror only grew and made her gasp for breath. The Union captain yanked her windbreaker down so hard that the zipper gave away with a rip. He threw her beanie into the snow and searched Rebane's pockets with rough, powerful hands. She watched how the men carried Liva inside and the fight went out of her. All her strength drained like a balloon deflating.

Two Union soldiers in arctic camo escorted Rebane through the open gates. She looked over her shoulder at the ATV, which stood lifeless among the dunes, the empty sled still attached to the coupling hook.

Their breaths misted in the cold as they escorted the prisoner across the yard, the snow creaking under their boots. Rebane saw what looked like offices on the second floor. The lights were on. A man's silhouette drew sharp against the flooding light from the fluorescent tubes. He leaned his arm against the window frame and looked down at the group. A shudder went through Rebane.

It's all over.

The blood ebbed from her brain and the guard had to grab her elbow to save her from losing balance.

In her cell, she tried to calm down but instead felt panic rising again. Rebane rose to pace in her cage like a trapped animal. She looked at the small, barred window with a blank gaze. Outside, the gloomy winter's day had turned into an evening. The blizzard had ceased, and the snowflakes slowly floated down. She could tell by the sound of the sentry's combat boots that he'd finished his round around the courtyard. That was all Rebane could see of him from the window. In fifteen minutes, he would return.

She closed her eyes to listen. No cries echoed from a torture chamber, and wherever the hospital was—probably on the ground level—she could sense nothing of Liva. The heater hummed with a sleepy rhythm, and the panopticon surveillance camera observed her with its cold, black eye from its station in the ceiling.

Rebane dreaded each echo ringing through the basement corridor. Whenever a guard walked past, she expected him to stop outside her door. An eye would gaze in from the Judas hatch and the key would turn in the lock. Weisser would stand there filling the doorway with his solid form. Rebane remembered his eyes—cold and expressionless.

My life is over. I got one year of borrowed time—not a day more.

What she most hated was the memory of his smell. And Rebane didn't care for appearances anymore. After three hours in the cell, tears swam into her eyes. She folded on the bunk with sobs that shook her tired shoulders, and she wiped the snot into the blanket, which smelled of soap. The tears which she had held back now flooded with unstoppable pressure.

All she could do was pray.

Lady of The Woods,
We seek Your help in despair and danger.
Our hunters seek Your help.
You raise the game. You bring the bear to us as a gift.
For your help, the wives giving birth cry out. [4]

She startled upright when the retracting bolts of the door clanked.

No fight moves. No resistance this time.

She expected to face Weisser, with his eyes gleaming of victory behind his steel-rimmed glasses. Rebane decided to meet him with her eyes bright and alert.

Instead, an elderly warder with pouches under his eyes stood in the middle of her cell. He placed the keyring back onto his belt and waited for someone to appear. The man's eyes reflected curiosity as he studied the female prisoner from head to toe. The stiff-necked captain stepped in. Rebane managed to give him a look of fear and hate. Her heart now pounded in her throat as she tried to imagine which method of pain she would face first.

You'll take me to the torture chamber. So be it.

Outside, the yard was a sea of dark and the sentry had vanished.

The captain cleared his throat before uttering with brutal directness, "You're free to go, Miss Nordstrom." From his expression, Rebane read disappointment.

28.
Confrontation

The gates opened and a murmur walked among the guards who still considered Rebane dangerous. One of them, a man with a flat nose and hostile eyes, followed three feet behind her and pointed at the prisoner with his service pistol.

Is this a sham? A form of torture to get up my hopes?

Her head swam with confusion. The sky curved above, starless and obsidian black. Rebane halted outside the sphere of the airfield's floodlights because her eyes hadn't yet adjusted to the dark.

"Keep walking," flat-nosed commanded in broken Russian.

She obeyed. A spot between Rebane's shoulder blades itched with vulnerability.

Will they shoot me in the back now?

Her instinct forced her to turn. The man with the Glock stood in front of the guard shack—a silhouette against the floodlight. The gate closed with a clank of steel against steel. Rebane almost passed out with relief and searched for her own footprints to find the ATV. It was so cold it hurt and the wind amplified the crisp bite of the night air. Rebane gave up on the zipper of her parka and wrapped her belt on top of it.

I should have asked for my weapons.

Departing without the Tikka felt like betraying an old friend. The wry captain had thrown her jacket at her and the old warder had returned her bootstraps—and that was it. Her food, a change of clothing and everything else she'd carried remained with the enemy.

If I stumble into a wolf pack, there's nothing I can do to save myself.

Her stomach hardened when she tripped on the snowdrift, almost falling on top of the ATV. Rebane closed her eyes for a moment to see better in the dark. She tried getting the arctic cat running, but only the solenoid clicked as she turned the key. The motor never fired.

She unstrapped the skis which Khaled's men had attached to the ATV and fitted her boots on the binds. Rebane blew onto her fingertips to get the blood flow going before she put on the mittens. Her chest tingled when she wondered if Liva lay dead on the operating table amidst a pool of blood. Rebane held the ski sticks in her hand, unable to depart.

Maybe you'll travel home, Liva Lowe, wherever that is.

The clouds drifted apart, and Venus—the morning star, twinkled between the white-coated hills. The sky began to redden. A flock of hooded crows circled the watchtower.

Facing the remainder of the night, she threaded her hands through the pole loops. The snow creaked under someone's shoes, approaching fast.

The pain arrived without warning.

A blow slammed against her skull and made her go blank. Rebane lost balance and landed on her back in the snowdrift. She raised her arms instinctively before the second stroke hit her jaw. Her scream got caught in her throat.

"Open your eyes," Weisser said in a disembodied voice. His knee pressed against her chest.

Her blood pumped faster. His breathing grew a bit deeper as he took a fistful of Rebane's hair and yanked. "I told you to open your eyes."

As she obeyed, she faced her worst nightmare—who now sat astride on her stomach. Rebane thrashed to free her legs from the skis, but the binds only tightened. The fiberglass skis twisted her ankle tendons and prevented her from joining her feet around the bulk of him. The soft snow gave in beneath their combined weight and Rebane sank. His body relaxed for a moment because he noticed that her fight was useless. She struggled for breath.

"I let you live, and you never thanked me," he said in a familiar, colorless tone, locking his shark eyes with Rebane. Weisser looked the same, except older than she remembered. The breaking of the first light behind his broad shoulders left his face in the shadow. He had pouches under his eyes and tired lines from nose to chin which the lighting emphasized. Weisser was still paunchy in his midsection under the down parka, and his weight crushed her.

"Are you finished wiggling?" he asked with a solemn expression. "You can fight me if you want, but we both know how this will end." She could tell he was enjoying himself.

Rebane got her hand free from the pole loop and tore his fur-trimmed hood down, but Weisser's arms were longer than hers. He straightened himself and his face remained beyond her reach. The middle-aged man responded by cupping handfuls of snow and filling Rebane's nose and mouth with the frozen substance. Rebane shook her head, which only made him apply more pressure. She coughed and spluttered to get mouthfuls of oxygen between doses of rough-handed snow-washing. The ice had mixed with the snow and scratched her face.

"Stop!" she managed to gasp after spitting blood and snow.

"Are you going to behave?" Weisser asked, his hooded eyes narrowed into slits. Rebane could see he was enjoying one of his sweetest victories. His voice mirrored his self-assurance over a weaker opponent.

She coughed and tasted blood. "Yes. Just stop, please."

His glasses fogged from the fight, and it occurred to Rebane that he may not be able to see far without them.

"That's more like it, Miss Nordstrom," he added just before she grabbed his metal-rimmed eyeglasses and threw them into the snow. Rebane tore a tuft of his sand-colored hair, which made Weisser grunt, but his fingers found their way around her throat and started squeezing.

She managed to feel for the buckle of her boot with her fingers and opened one ankle strap. Rebane lifted a knee to kick his side. But Weisser knew all her moves from before. He caught her leg in the fork of his forearm and pushed up. Rebane screamed as the tendons of her thigh stretched beyond their capacity. In a last desperate attempt, Rebane tried to grab the sidearm he wore in a belt holster, but Weisser twisted her hand and the bones in her wrist caused such agony that she gave up.

"Fuck you!" she screamed because of the pain and because she had nothing else to throw at him.

"I just might," he purred. "For old time's sake."

The old fear flared up. Rebane concentrated on her breathing because his weight restricted the movement of her ribcage. Weisser looked disappointed that she didn't give him the resistance he had expected. His eyes were clear and cold. The colonel gazed over his shoulder to make sure no one would disturb them.

When he looked at Rebane again, he tilted his head. "I saw my bit of action when we captured the Eastern Zones during the Nuclear War. War is no place for little girls who think they can join the big boys' club. You know what we did to Russian bitches like you after we marched into a conquered city?"

Rebane knew she wouldn't like the story but remained silent. She stared at him with an unrestrained, animal-like terror.

No help will arrive. Let him talk. Buy time.

"We fucked them until there was a puddle of blood between their legs. Sometimes we raped the girls in front of their families. You should have seen them squirm." His soft laughter was without humor. "And sometimes we used our knives."

Rebane had seen her share of atrocities. She had looked the other way—concentrated on her mission. Weisser's words resurrected memories of the corpses with their skirts drawn up and their bruised legs left open. The smell of rotting flesh everywhere...

Weisser straightened his back and towered above her. The strap of his gun holster snapped open. He drew the Glock slowly, his breath puffing as clouds in the dawning light. Rebane lay paralyzed, staring into the black eye of the barrel.

You must act. Fight him!

But her breath stopped, and her heart sank. Her eyes widened with fear as Rebane understood that her limbs wouldn't obey.

"You always had a special place in my heart, Rebane," he said as he ran his tongue across his upper teeth. "You know that don't you?" Weisser's eyes beamed when he put his left hand on her throat to keep Rebane in place. She flinched as the barrel of the Glock pressed against her forehead. "But I cannot let you get away with treason. It would mean I could no longer do my job, that I'm not capable of the hardness it demands of me," he continued in a calm voice.

Rebane tried to turn her head. Her body shook from the cold that seeped through her clothes. She expected the 9mm bullet to blast her skull into splinters from such a close range. Her brain searched for the words which would make him spare her life a second time, but only a muffled "No," came out. She didn't dare move because he had his finger on the trigger.

"I could kill you with my bare hands," he leaned over to whisper, "but you need artillery to defeat me." His short hair ruffled in the wind. It had started to turn grey above his ears.

It's all over.

Rebane's breath rose in a mist before her. She concentrated her thoughts on Liva and the sweet baby the young mother would now be rocking against her bosom. Rebane wanted a happy memory to be her last, not the stench of the man who sat on top of her.

Her vision blurred and Weisser became a flickering shadow. She only saw the barrel of the Glock in detail. The hold on her throat loosened and she managed to turn her head to the side. The explosion rang in the frigid air, sliced her ears with pain. Something wet poured over her cheeks with warmth, on her chest...

And the smell of gunpowder lingered. Rebane managed to roll on her side just before she expelled vomit.

Then everything faded. She blacked out.

Weisser still lay on top of her, slackened and enormous. Someone slapped her cheek. "Rebane! Wake up. I can't use my abdominal muscles because of the C-section," the angelic voice rang. "You must get him off you! We must go before the guards find out I'm gone."

Rebane lay rigid with shock and thought, I'm dead.

She decided not to move, but the voice wouldn't give up.

"Bitch! Coward! You can't give up now. We need you." The voice grew angry and high-pitched. Because the slapping stung her face and Rebane feared another hit, she opened her eyes, blinking the water away. The image of Liva wearing nothing but a paper gown from the hospital eventually grew focused. The youngster's teeth clattered together from the cold. A draft penetrated Rebane's body.

Liva tried to bend, to lift a bundle from the snow. "Aargh," I can't. Reb, help. She'll freeze on the ground. Give the baby to me." It took a moment before Rebane could focus on Liva. The sunrise crowned her head with a halo.

"Am I dead?" Rebane muttered to herself.

"No, you're not dead, silly. But we all will be if you don't move soon. I'm freezing. Can't you see I need clothes? Give his winter coat to me. It looks warm." When Rebane didn't move, Liva added, "Unless you want to wear them and give me yours." Rebane noticed the sparkle of humor in the youngster's eyes.

Rebane grunted to reach the remaining ski bind. "Can't you at least open the buckle?"

"No."

"Fuck!" She cursed as she squirmed under Weisser's massive carcass, which was still warm. His chubby face was red with cold. He looked alive. By the time she managed to push him by the shoulders and worm her way out from underneath him, Rebane had swallowed a lot of blood-soaked snow. She spluttered and coughed, bending double. Her steps were as unsure as a sleepwalker's, but Rebane picked up the baby with careful hands. Just a pink bulb of a nose stuck out from the bundle of tightly wrapped blankets and sheets which the mother had stolen in a hurry. Liva opened her arms and Rebane's heartbeat quickened with joy. The baby yawned and the mother offered the girl her pinkie. Tiny lips suckled her fingertip.

As Rebane struggled to roll Weisser on his back, she fixed her gaze on the handle of a surgical scalpel that stuck out from his throat. She kneeled to open his coat zipper, staying as far away as she could, scared that he would reanimate, and those enormous hands would smother whatever life was left inside of her.

Liva hopped from one bare leg to the other and assured her, "Don't worry. A healer knows where to stick a pig like him." The girl hugged the baby with bloody hands—the see-through hospital gown bathed in bright-red spatter. The morning sun highlighted Liva with rose gold. Without the blood covering her, the girl would have been the epitome of the Madonna. With Rebane's assistance, Liva threaded one skinny arm into the sleeve of Weisser's parka and then another.

"Did you kill him?» Rebane›s voice still seethed with disbelief. She had gathered enough courage to take a closer look at Weisser.

"Yes! Who else would have saved your sissy ass—again? Now, shoes and trousers, please. Do I have to guide you through every move?"

I don't want to touch him.

But then again, Rebane didn't want to give up her own clothes. The sun rose from behind the crust of a hill that covered the view to the airbase and Rebane understood why they must hurry. She looked away as she opened the dead man's belt. He still smelled of his cigarette brand, something Rebane didn't want to remember.

I, a trained soldier, was so helpless with him, and that string bean of a woman could take his life with one sting?

"Because I didn't know him." Liva's voice rang almost angelic. The baby made a little yelping noise and then fell asleep while Liva resumed her rocking motion. "He ruled you with terror and violence. You're in shock because of the trauma he caused you. Don't feel bad about it because I do. The medicine woman shouldn't kill," Liva continued. "It's an offense against Mielikki, who is the high priestess of all healers. This big monster," she gestured toward Weisser's corpse, "he never saw me coming because he was so preoccupied with you. I walked barefooted toward your screams."

The windshield of the ATV had covered with frost. A gust of wind loosened a veil of snow from the dune. "I didn't cry! I fought him tooth and nail," Rebane exclaimed, offended. "And why the fuck didn't you wear shoes? Your big toe looks as if it needs amputation." She regretted her anger immediately and the redness of shame surfaced on her skin.

"Duh! I sneaked away as soon as I woke from the narcosis and they put the baby on my breasts," Liva explained. She had emptied Weisser's pockets and found his cold weather gloves and knit hat. "Perhaps the nurse thought I was still sleepy—she was nice, by the way—and they left me without a guard. But I didn't waste time searching for my clothes."

"How did you get out past the guards?"

"I have no idea. I couldn't see in the pitch black so I followed the footprints in the snow. When I lost track—the wind had covered the path and my toes had lost all feeling—Mielikki took my hand. She guided me on top of the dune where I saw the blink of the man's headlamp before he put it out."

"Thank you, *Meine Freundin*," Rebane muttered more to herself than to Liva. She cringed at the thought of what could have happened without Liva's intervention. "Liva and...uh hum baby, sit in the toboggan. I must open the strap locks and cut the sled loose from the ATV."

"Aurora. Her name is Aurora," Liva said, her narrow face beaming with pride. The shade of pink had returned to her lips, which reminded Rebane of rose petals. The fierce, passionate eyes were full of tenderness and she smoothed her hair. "Damn. He ruined my hairdo. Help me get into the sled."

Liva cried out when she lowered herself into the toboggan, even when Rebane supported most of her weight with her arms linked on Liva's chest.

"I'm sorry you hurt so much," Rebane said as she handed Aurora to Liva. "Put her inside the down parka. That will leave your hands free and she'll stay warm."

"I'll heal if the stitches hold, Liva said, her large eyes mirroring the perfect blue of the sky. " I think the surgeon did a good job." All her vulnerability was gone. "Now ski for your life, Nenets nomad, if we want to catch up to Khaled and Bjorn."

"Do you know where the group is headed?" Rebane turned to look at Liva when she closed the buckles of the pulling harness with a series of clicks.

"Yes. Bjorn told me when he strapped me onto the sled." Liva knotted Weisser's hood strings and held onto the wooden beam of the toboggan. "I'm ready if you are." The teenager flashed a smile which competed with the winter sun.

Quotations and Sources

1. The poems and snippets from old Finnish legends quoted in part from: http://www.finnishmyth.org/FINNISH_MYTHS_CULTS/   Research, God and Cult Texts, Poems and translations of poems from trad. texts by Reijo Nenonen.

2. A poem from traditional Finnish myths, translated and modified by the author.

3. The poems and snippets from old Finnish legends quoted in part from: http://www.finnishmyth.org/FINNISH_MYTHS_CULTS/   Research, God and Cult Texts, Poems and translations of poems from trad. texts by Reijo Nenonen.

4. A poem from traditional Finnish myths, translated and modified by the author.

Besides *Unholy Warrior*, Finnish author Rebecka Jäger co-authored the well-received satire, *Romance Kills*, and Book one of the Cursed and the Damned series, *Conjuror of Evil*.

Born in the Northern part of Finland, known as Lapland, she embraced the arctic temperatures and became an avid musher and highly skilled markswoman—a necessary skill when hunting for food. She studied history at the University of Helsinki and screenwriting at Aalto University's Department of Film, Television, and Scenography.

She wrote professional texts throughout her career but decided to learn the delicate art of writing fiction later on. She mastered the craft in different writer's workshops—always keen to become a better writer.

Her work ranges from dystopian to historical and stays mostly within the thriller genre. Arctic nature is a recurring theme in her writing.

As a dedicated fan of action-packed novels, she loves Tom Clancy and Robert Ludlum, but also the subtle way of building suspense used by the ultimate grand-master of spy novels—John LeCarre. Her favorite writer will always be George Orwell with his bone-chilling *1984*: an evergreen classic of dystopian literature.

https://rebeckajager.com
https://twitter.com/JagerWriter
www.instagram.com/rebeckajager
https://www.facebook.com/rebeckajagerwriter

Lightning Source UK Ltd.
Milton Keynes UK
UKHW020642161220
375314UK00013B/422/J